Gerald Locklin

The Pocket Book

A Novella
and Nineteen Short Fictions

Water Row Press
Sudbury
2003

Grateful acknowledgement is made to California State University, Long Beach for support of the writing of parts of this book in the form of assigned time.

Water Row Press
PO Box 438
Sudbury MA, 01776
waterrow@aol.com
www.waterrowbooks.com
write for free catalogue

ISBN 0-934953-77-5
Printed in USA
Book design and typesetting by Henri Hadida

Library of Congress Cataloging-in-Publication Data
Locklin, Gerald.
The pocket book: a novella and nineteen short fictions/
Gerald Locklin
p.cm
ISBN 0-934953-77-5
I. Title.

PS3562.O265P63 2003
d813'.54--dc21

2003041160

Dedication

Jeffrey Weinberg
Tim Grobaty
Dr. Martin Bax
Marilyn Johnson
Barbara Hauk
Joan Jobe Smith
David Caddy
Joseph Shields
Jerry Hagins
Jules Smith
Shane Rhodes
Tim Wells

This book is,
in its entirety, a work of fiction.

Table of Contents

Short Fictions

The Pocket Book

He is lined up across from the All-American Tight End, Whizzer Quisenberry. His back aches; his gut nearly touches the ground; his arms have grown thin as chopsticks. But though he has the ailments of middle-age, he retains the instincts of a whippersnapper. He anticipates the hike-count, sidesteps Quisenberry, and is in the enemy backfield a fraction of a second after the football. He does not have the strength to tackle the young stud, but he is heavy enough to slow him down until his teammates can arrive. Together they pile on the runner's back until his knees touch the ground. The gun goes off for halftime.

It does not strike him as strange that both teams picnic together at halftime. Most are thoroughly congenial, but Quisenberry eyes him maliciously. He tries to return the look with the quiet confidence evinced by Shane eyeball-to-eyeball with Jack Wilson. It ain't as easy outside the realm of legend. He glances at the scoreboard which shows a minus-six to minus-six tie. That does strike him as strange because he can remember learning that minus-numbers do not exist in reality, that the minus sign is only indicative of an operation to be performed. Something drastic is called for—a drastic tactic. In the first huddle of the second half, he stage-whispers, "Quick-Kick!" And when the quarterback does not veto the play, he drops back himself in punt-formation. You can imagine his elation when he handles the hike handily and kicks the ball completely out of the stadium. Let Quisenberry put that one in his pipe and smoke it . . .

It is only fair that he volunteer to retrieve the football himself. In the street outside the stadium he encounters a man and woman wearing enormous Alf Landon buttons. He asks them if they saw a football land. They say No, they did not see a football land, but they did see an unidentified flying object. He asks them if it was flying. No, they say, it was landed. Then how, he wishes to know, did they know it could fly? And if it couldn't fly, how could it be an unidentified flying object? Wouldn't it, in fact, be more precise to say they saw an unidentified landed object? And is it not true that they are from Kansas? Yes, they admit, they are from Kansas, but this is California, isn't it? He seems to remember that it is California, but nonetheless, is it not significant that it is only people from Kansas and Mississippi who see flying saucers? Or landed saucers? And would they by any chance know if they were born vaginally or by Caesarean section? They do not know the answer to that, nor do they see the significance of it. It is significant, he says. What is the significance, they demand of him. He cannot remember the significance of it, although he does remember that the way one is born is significant to the hallucinations one later experiences. To distract attention from his momentary lapse, he points at his football, which he now sees sitting in the street. "Look." he cries,"there is my football. It's the one I won at the Saturday Cartoon Festival at Loew's theatre, and it was the first and last thing I ever won at any festival, and when I got it home it turned out to be so chintzy that the wind would carry it away. I had won an utterly useless football. And there it now sits."

The folks from Kansas correct him: "That is not a football. That is an Unidentified Flying Object." As fate would have it, the football has landed right in front of his girlfriend's apartment. He goes to her door and stands there a minute before knocking. When he is sure he does not hear any bedsprings or heavy breathing, he knocks. She peeks out at him before removing the chain.

"Hi," he says, "I was just in the neighborhood and thought I'd stop by."

"I'm glad you did," she says; "It's been six weeks since I've seen you."

"I know," he says. "And I know that the last time I saw you I said I'd be back the next day. But I had forgotten some errands that I had to run. You haven't been unfaithful to me, have you?"

"Of course not," she says. "Don't be paranoid."

"And you didn't mind sitting home waiting for me for six weeks, did you?"

"No. It was a privilege."

"I'm glad you feel that way. It makes our relationship function much more smoothly than if you chose to behave like a prima donna. Now, speaking of functions how would you like to perform a sexual function."

"I'd like to," she says. "Just let me spend a minute in the bathroom,"

A minute later she emerges from the bathroom in tears: "I'm so embarrassed," she says. "I know this is going to spoil everything."

"Probably not. Tell me what's the trouble."

"I was removing my tampon and the string broke,"

"Not to worry, my dear. We'll have it out in a jiffy."

"You mean you've had experience with this sort of thing?"

"Not exactly. But I did earn my certificate in Cardio-Pulmonary Resuscitation. Just lie back down on the bed and try to relax."

He administers CPR for a good twenty minutes, but somehow this fails to dislodge the tampon. Finally he just sticks a couple of fingers up there, not for the first time, and manages to get behind the tampon and force it out, He tosses it nonchalantly in the waste basket and goes to wash his hands with the jaunty air of a brain surgeon celebrating a successful operation.

"Oh, thank you."

"It was nothing."

"But now you'll be . . . turned off."

"My dear", he says, basking in the glow of his own magnanimity, "nothing human is alien to me."

At the door, he says, "I'll be back tomorrow. You'll be waiting faithfully, won't you?"

"Oh yes."

"And if something comes up and I can't make it back here tomorrow?"

"I'll just wait until the next day."

"I don't want to feel I'm a millstone upon your young life, I wouldn't want you to sacrifice your life to my pleasure unless I was sure that was what you felt was best for you."

"I do, I'm perfectly happy."

"I'm glad to hear it. If you weren't the guilt would be too much for me to bear. I can't allow guilt to become a distraction for me. I'd have to stop seeing you."

"Oh, please don't ever jump to that horrible conclusion."

"Then I will hope to see you on the morrow."

He decides to have a beer across the street.

There he runs into an old friend who is now retired wealthy at the age of forty from owning a construction business. They talk about the UCLA-Michigan State Rose Bowl game in which Bob Stiles stopped the Hawaiian fullback Bob Apisa on the UCLA one-yard line. They talk about the guy they knew who once crashed the Johnny Carson Show. The stage, not the audience. And the friend says that that guy is now a frequenter of the Playboy mansion and recently took him there as a guest. The friend describes some of the sexual excesses he witnessed there and adds,

"I could probably get you an invitation, but I know you wouldn't like it."

"Once a philosopher."

"No, no, it's all very degrading, especially to the women. You wouldn't want to feel you'd been a part of anything misogynistic, anything that involved the sexual humiliation of women."

"No, but still...

"I wouldn't do it to you. I wouldn't do it to your work."

"I don't think that just going there one time would...

"No, I won't hear of it. I wouldn't take the responsibility for the corruption of your talent. That's the last time we will even talk of it. Instead, why don't we see if I can get a couple of decent seats for the USC-Notre Dame game."

He returns to his one-bedroom apartment. His wife has finished putting the children in bed, finished the dishes, poured herself a dark brew, and is looking at a magazine. He has been watching a pro basketball game, but it has just ended and, since no act can follow the mercury-tongued announcer, Chick Hearn, he has turned off the t.v.

"What are you reading?" he asks his wife.

"None of your fucking business," she replies.

"Did I pay for half of that magazine subscription?"

"No, you refused to. You said it was aimed at the intelligence of an educationally deprived pterodactyl."

"Oh."

He picks up the financial section of the paper. A stock he recently inherited a few shares of has dropped ten points in five days.

She has put down her magazine and has picked up some knitting.

'What're you knitting?" he asks,

"None of your fucking business," she replies.

"Didn't I pay for half of that yarn?"

"No, you said you'd only pay for it if I promised to knit myself a noose."

"Oh."

He turns to the astrology column in the newspaper. Under his sign, Aquarius, he reads, "You may encounter difficulties communicating with your mate. Get out of the house. A movie may fill the bill."

He folds his copy of the Herald-Excalibur neatly, as she has trained him to do, and slides it under the bookcase. "I'm going out for a while," he says.

"Who gives a fuck?"

"Unless you'd rather I stayed home and when you're finished with your knitting of whatever it is you're knitting we could maybe screw."

"Don't be ridiculous." she says

"You wouldn't feel a little safer with me here with you?"

"Are you kidding? What would you do to protect me?"

"I earned a green belt in karate."

"Yeah, sixteen years ago."

"Won't the kids maybe miss me if they wake up in the night?"

"The kids don't care if you come or go, live or die. The kids only care about their mother."

"But I thought we were living in a patriarchy?"

"Wake up; the middle ages ended yesterday."

"Oh. Well I guess I'll go catch a movie then."

"There's one at the theatre on Main Street that should be just right for you."

"Oh yeah? What's it called?"

"It's called The Decline of Western Civilization."

The ticket vendor at the movie theatre asks him,

"Are you sure you know what this film is all about, sir?"

"I don't have the foggiest."

"Then how do you know you won't be offended?"

"Because anything alien is human to me,"

"Okay, but absolutely no refunds.'

"I wouldn't think of it."

On his way to the counter he overhears an angry woman demanding her money back. The ticket vendor is telling her, "Why not?" The woman behind the concession counter asks what he would like.

"Coke will be fine."

"Small or large?"

"Small."

With a razor blade she creates a thin line of white powder on the counter.

"What's that?"

"Your coke, of course."

"Oh, how much is it?"

"Twenty dollars."

"I don't have twenty dollars. Would you take a personal check or credit card?"

"Hell, no," she says, "but watch this..."

She hikes her skirt up above her hips and sits back on her high stool. She is wearing a white garter belt, white stockings, but no panties. With her left hand she parts her vaginal lips, while she moistens the finger of her right hand with her tongue, scoops the coke back up with it, and rubs it gently an her clitoris. "Oh my god," she moans.

He vaults the counter, situates himself between her thighs, and unzips his throbbing member. He is about to penetrate her when they are joined by the ticket vendor who is shouting, "Cut: All customers into the theatre: All theatre personnel at battle stations! The film is about to begin!"

He zips back up and goes to take the second seat in the last row of the auditorium.

He has, as usual, brought a half-pint of vodka in his jacket pocket. He would prefer something to mix it with but doesn't dare return to the concession counter. The first couple of gulps burn his esophagus, but the next couple numb it. He is beginning to feel almost happy.

The movie is a series of very loud punk rock bands. In one of the first there is a man named Darby Crash who cannot seem to remember to sing into the microphone or to keep from falling down on stage. The people in the bands and on the stage have cut their hair and painted themselves to resemble white Indians on the warpath.

Many have violated their noses or earlobes with sharp objects. They are trying very hard to look fierce.

A funny story is told of a dead painter in somebody's backyard.

During filmed performances of the group

called Black Flag there are riots by the patrons inside and the police outside.

A producer explains that the number of beats per minute are deliberately increased to where the music cannot be danced to in anything but the most violent fashion and where feelings of violence will be stirred in the audience. At this point a young man appears from where he has been slouched in the front row of the theatre and begins shouting obscenities and racing up and down the aisles. He scowls and curses but does not make good any of his threats. After a while he returns to the front row where he once again slouches out of sight.

The best group musically and in terms of lyrics is called X. Their names are John Doe and Exene and Don Bonebrake and Billy Zoom. Billy Zoom is a very normal looking person, which makes him an eccentric in this movie.

Various young people looking quite far gone are interviewed as to the significance of this music and the appearance and behavior of the people who go out to listen to it. Their comments seem to indicate that it is related to the world in which they are living, but they are not very specific.

The last group, Fear, abuses their audience with homosexual epithets. People try to leap onto the stage, but are hurled back off by bouncers. Dancers bounce like pogo sticks and slam into each other,

Someone slips into the auditorium and takes

the seat next to him. It is the woman from behind the concession counter. She runs her fingernails up the inside of his thighs to his fly and expertly opens his pants, She yanks free in her hand his stiffening member and, with her other hand, applies a white powder to the head of it. "Oh god," he groans and, sinking his fists into her hair, attempts to draw her mouth down to
it . . .

"Cut!"

The screen goes blank and the lights go on.

"Film's over! Everybody out!"

Already the concession stand lady has disappeared. There is no sign of the man from the front row. The only other people leaving the theatre are two children coming towards him up the aisle. He recognizes them as his daughter and son, fifteen and twelve, by his second wife.

He hurries to put himself away and rises to embrace them. "What are you guys doing here?"

"You always told us not to be afraid of knowledge," his daughter says.

"Did you like the film?"

"It was interesting," his daughter said. "The story about the dead painter made me laugh."

"It was too loud," his son says. "I kept my fingers in my ears."

"Did that wild man in the aisles scare you?"

"A little. He didn't touch us though."

'How did you get here?"

"We took the bus."

"Forty-five miles?"
"I read."
"I did my rubik's cube."
"Well, let me give you a ride home," he says.

His second wife says, "I thought the movie was playing in San Clemente. Thanks for bringing them home."

"No problem," he says.

She walks him to his car while they discuss the best time for the kids to visit him again. "I'm hoping to get to Mexico for a few days soon," she says.

"Do you remember when I took you to Mexico City and we had only been going out for two weeks, and it was only a week since I'd separated from my first wife and my first three kids?"

"How could I forget? Would anyone else have spent fifty bucks on round-trip bus tickets for two between T.J. and Mexico City? You were always a big spender."

"The hotel room by the railroad station in Guadalajara only cost a buck a night."

"And turned out to be where the whores brought their customers. And the walls were covered with roaches."

"But we didn't bother them and they didn't bother us. What was the name of that kid we met on the bus who was trying to get over the girl he'd just broken up with but after the roach-ridden brothel-hotel by the railway station he flew back home to her?"

"His name was John.

"He really liked you."

"You were jealous of everyone who ever looked twice at me."

"You have a way of making your men jealous."

"I've never been unfaithful to a man I was committed to. You just have a way of making yourself jealous. And what a hypocrite—you were unfaithful to me every chance you got."

"It was the only way I could distract myself from insane jealousy. And I wasn't unfaithful to you on that trip to Mexico."

"No, I suppose that's true. You weren't unfaithful to me until after we were married, were you?'

"No, do you think I suffer from the virgin/whore syndrome that Doctor Toni Grant of KABC talk-radio says afflicts almost all American men?"

"I think you suffer from everything that a man could suffer from and not be locked up."

"Do you think I let the incest taboo slop over into my relationship with my wives?"

"No I think you just felt trapped. And that you were too young to be trapped. And that you'd fall-en twice for the same trap. We had good sex after marriage."

"But maybe less good after you became a mother?"

"Maybe . . . sometimes, though..."

"I was lousy that first night that we went to bed. I was afraid I'd never get it up again. And you stuck with me until everything was fine. I wanted to fuck you day in and day out then . . . you had the most beautiful tits that I've seen on a small girl to this very day . . . I was so grateful to you that I made myself a vow that I would never hurt you,"

"You broke that one with a vengeance."

"I nursed you through that terrible virus in Mexico City."

"What would you have done if I'd died on you with my parents thinking I was staying with some mythical Maria Hidalgo Hernandez in Hermosillo?"

"I kept my mind off that by reading William Carlos Williams. I read Paterson for the first time at the side of your sickbed. And I ran back and forth bringing you cold soft drinks from the supermercado."

"Until you came down with turista yourself."

"I thought I'd never pass another truly formed stool. It was months, in fact, before I felt safe enough to walk around with a partially relaxed sphincter."

"And that American doctor whose name we got from the American Embassy didn't want to have anything to do with us because we weren't legally married."

"The summer of 1965."

"But as soon as I was feeling better we went to

the races at the Hippodrome, sitting in the clubhouse and eating these enormous platters of mashed potatoes,"

"Purée de patates."

"Everything was so cheap then."

"I spent my last eight hundred bucks of savings in six weeks."

"We stayed in the cheapest hotels and drank in the most expensive hotel bars."

"On the Reforma. Cuba libres. And tipped the mariachis."

"After we got sick we had to eat in expensive restaurants too."

"I still can't face enchiladas de pollo con mole poblano. Although I had probably already doomed myself with those chicken tacos at that stand in Tepic in the middle of the night-long bus ride from Mazatlan. Or else it was those comidas downtown in Guadalajara. But I enjoyed those meals."

"And the parque azul."

"And the chateaubriand for two at the French restaurant on the Reforma."

"And the pasta and Caesar salad prepared at the table."

"And all the drinks and music."

"Every night."

"But it was so hard to hold one's head up drinking after we got sick."

"Especially at the Mexico City altitude.'

'We should have gone to the pyramids."

"We didn't feel well enough. And I had to get back to teach summer school."

"We didn't get to Cuernavaca or Taxco or San Miguel de Allende."

"We got to Xochimilco and it sucked."

"You pronounced it ex-otch-y-milko and wondered why no one could tell us how to get there."

"I learned."

"The police were always nice to us."

"Just about everyone was. The cabbies at the bus station tried to rip us off and get kickbacks by taking us to an expensive hotel, but we'd been warned by that friend of yours . . . what was his name?"

"His name was John too,"

"He was hot to get into your pants."

'You were always insanely . . . "

"No, he and I got drunk together the night before you and I left on the trip and he admitted it to me. That same night I pedalled him home on the handlebars of a bicycle with flat tires. He had hopes right up till we got married of beating me out for you. So did the other John, the pianist who was the nephew of the famous painter. He came by my house ostensibly to demonstrate an oxy-acetylene torch he'd just bought and then he insisted that we go and pick you up and bring you back to meet my wife and kids because he wanted to see if we would let on that we were in love and he thought that bringing you into the domestic ménage might break us up. And then I stopped by on a hunch that day when he was trying to pressure you, and I carried you off like a knight."

"We never hear of any of these talented young people. None of them ever made it,"

"That one black actor made it. But we didn't know him well."

"You had your moments. You took me away from that big black athlete who cut in on us at the end-of-semester party up the hill from school."

"That was the first time we went out, And it was pure chance our paths crossed. I was on my way from my office to my car and you and the black-haired girl were sitting on the lawn and she made some good-natured fun of me and I wandered over to chat and you guys talked me into at least stopping by at the party."

"And when you called home to say you'd be late for dinner, your wife hung up on you."

"So I said I'd might as well hang for a sheep as a goat and we stayed out till after the bars closed,"

"You took me to that tinny neighborhood place in Alhambra and introduced me to gin-and-tonics,"

'Thirty-five cents each."

"And we hugged and kissed in the phony-leather booth."

"And afterwards I had you down under me on the front seat of my car, but you said no so I didn't."

"But you tried enough times to get me to say yes instead of no."

"It was very exciting."

"A week later we were rolling around in the wet grass at Griffith Park."

"But you still wouldn't let me go all the way. The grass stains were the last straw when I got home though. My wife flew home to her parents two days later."

"And that night I borrowed my-older-brother-the lawyer's mustang to come meet you and you took me to your apartment off of Valley Boulevard and you plied me with chianti and a couple of hours of excruciating foreplay…"

"I kept pulling down your pants, and you kept pulling them back up. You said your mother always told you not to take your pants off at a man's apartment."

"But finally I left them down and we went into your bedroom…"

"And I had trouble then, overpreparation of the event, no doubt, and wanting you so bad, I thought I'd have to go to a psychiatrist, but you said, Nonsense, and you just applied yourself to remedying the problem…"

"And by morning it was clear that everything was going to be all right."

"And we drove to Malibu for breakfast. Which is a long ride from the San Gabriel Valley."

"And a few days later we were on a bus from Tijuana to Mexico City, with stops in Guaymas, Mazatlan and Guadalajara."

"The first leg was the worst. Nearly twenty-four hours and the Sonora desert steaming in the middle of the summer."

"Guaymas was beautiful though—the deep blue bay surrounded by white desert hills."

"I insisted on making love as soon as we were in our room. You were hot and tired but I couldn't resist your body then. I'd never seen such lovely breasts, especially on anyone that small."

"And I pretended I couldn't swim and let you try to teach me."

"And I didn't realize how quickly you can burn on Mexican beaches in the summer. If I'd been burned a little worse we would have had to turn back for the states."

"And in Mazatlan the room with the overhead fan at the old beach and Tom Collinses on the patio in the heat of the afternoon and, at sunset, the strolls along the promenade."

"And The Shrimp Bucket before it became famous."

"You got angry at me at dinner because I'd made a joke at your expense in front of the men who'd joined us at the table and up in the room you hurled the travelers cheques at me and told me to go home."

"I'm sure that I was bluffing but I don't think that I knew I was."

"You got away with it. I didn't leave. Were you bluffing the first time that I caught you cheating after we were married and you said you guessed we'd better split up because you were starting to wander, and I asked you if you couldn't like me and other women too, and so you said you'd try?"

"No, I really thought we should split up then."

"We lived together three more years,"

"And separately but still married for another six or seven. My present wife says I go for the jugular."

"Maybe it doesn't work with her. It always worked with me."

"Was it in Mazatlan we had the trouble in the dive?"

"No, that was Guadalajara. You said I caused it by talking to the big Mexican who said he was from Los Angeles and who wanted to talk to me."

"I'm capable of paranoia, God knows, but that wasn't paranoia."

"You told him that he couldn't dance with me and then he came back from the kitchen with an envelope for you and when you opened it a toy grasshopper flew up and all the whores laughed at you."

"We were lucky to get out of that place alive. Did you know that the kid with us was carrying a switchblade?"

"No."

"Well, he was. He showed it to me while the big Mexican was talking to you. I'm sure he'd never used one in his life and I was afraid that if he pulled it out in that place someone would get their hands on it and stick it up his ass. Or mine."

"Back at the hotel you quoted Raymond

Chandler to me."

"From The Fine Art of Murder, Philip Marlowe's creed, that he would suffer no man's insolence without a due and dispassionate revenge and that his pride was that you will treat him as a proud man or be very sorry that you ever saw him."

"I remember you were very upset. You'd insisted on staying in the bar for three more rounds, drinking yours and mine, just so it wouldn't seem that we'd been frightened away."

"I tried to explain to you that I believed as Marlowe did about what a man should strive to be, even though I was just a teacher and a writer, not a private eye."

"Do you still believe it?"

"A part of me does."

"You said you wanted to be such a man, not just to read and write about him,"

"I had a great belief in will power."

"Do you still?"

"I don't know."

"Anyway," he says, "you bit my nipples and I arched like a wounded sailfish and you convinced me with your body that you loved me and that I was still a man in your eyes."

"You arched like a wounded sailfish?"

"It's a phrase from a novel I wrote about that

summer many years ago. But I was so poor then that I couldn't afford a xerox copy and the original got lost in the mail to a publisher. At first I figured it was all for the best, because I had lost the confidence in my ability ever to write a novel. But later, when I'd had a few things published and some of them were from the same period as that book of the summer of 1965, I was no longer sure that what had been lost was without value."

"And then one day I was the wife. I told you you didn't have to marry me."

"I wanted to marry you, I would have gone to any lengths to have you,"

"We went to lengths. The elopement. . .

"To Tijuana. And I discover halfway down the P.C.H. that you've left a note for your parents identical with the one the girl was forced to leave in The Collector."

"I thought you were a god,"

"And I thought you had no respect for me.'

"Don't worry, I learned you were not a god."

He drives back up the San Diego Freeway listening to first a restaurant talk show and then a financial one. As he turns left onto Main Street back in his own home town he notices that The Decline of Western Civilization has been taken down from the marquee and a new title is going up, the first word of which is Confessions.

Confessions of what? he wonders.

Confessions of St. Augustine?

He takes from his glove compartment a handy guide to the movies and finds listed:

Confessions of a Nazi Spy

Confessions of a Police Captain

Confessions of a Window Cleaner

Confessions of an Opium Eater (a tale of slave girls)

Confessions of Boston Blackie

Confessions of Felix Krull

Confessions of Tom Harris (underrated prize-fighting tale)

also Confessions, The Confession, and Confess, Dr. Corda.

He parks his car and wanders up to the ticket window. "One, please."

"That will be five dollars."

"Incidentally, what's the name of the film—Confessions of What?

"Confessions-Five Dollars, But it's not a film. It's real, live, on-stage.'

"A real priest?"

"Well, you know, once a priest always a priest. The Indelible Sacramental Character, and all that. You better get inside; the first performance is just about to begin."

The house is full and the lights are dim. There is enthusiastic applause as the man in black steps onto the stage. As the priest takes the microphone

to his lips to summon the first volunteer from the audience, Jimmy gasps,
"Father Black." Then louder, "Whizzer!"

The priest's expression changes as he tries to peer to the back of the auditorium: "Who dares address his priest in such a manner?"

"It's me, Father Black, Jimmy Abbey! You remember St. Elmo's parish, the early '50's-"

"Jimmy! How wonderful to see you after so long! Come on up here and let the parishioners of the night get a look at you."

Jimmy climbs up on the stage and the priest puts an arm around his shoulder, "Folks, this is one of my oldest and dearest friends, James Abbey. I knew him when he was a gawky center on St. Elmo's eighth grade basketball team."

Polite applause from the congregation.

"Jimmy, I'd love to have a nice long chat with you, but since we were just about to get underway, perhaps you'd care to have a seat in the wings until intermission."

"I guess I'm in no rush. In fact, I don't even know what time it is."

"But you're wearing a watch."

"Yes, but I notice the hands are moving backwards."

"Well, it's a pretty cheap watch."

"I guess I got what I paid for."

"That's more than a lot of people can say. But my congregation is about to get the evening's first dose of what they paid for."

The priest enters a wooden confessional, center-stage, and takes a seat. He rests his elbow on the little shelf just inside the window, and rests his forehead in the palm of his hand.

The first penitent-volunteer rises from the audience and climbs the side steps to the stage. She is properly attired in a white, high-necked dress, and wears a white lace kerchief pinned to her Irish-black hair. As she crosses the stage on high heels, she appears an attractive early-thirties. She clutches a rosary and she kneels at the window of the three-sided confessional:

Penitent: Bless me, Father, for I have sinned

Confessors: God bless you, daughter . . .

Penitent: It has been… two weeks…since my last confession.

Confessor: Yes, my daughter.

Penitent: I was disobedient . . . about five or six times a day . . . and …

Confessor: Wait a second. Disobedient? Disobedient to whom?

Penitent: Uh… to my daddy.

Confessor: Your daddy? My god, that's horrible, that's the unforgivable sin!

Penitent: Yes, Daddy.

Confessors: Yes, FATHER:

Penitent: Yes, FATHER: Excuse me, FATHER:

Confessor: Go on, my daughter

Penitent: And I told five lies…
Confessor: Hold it. How many lies?
Penitent: Five.
Confessor: Five exactly?
Penitent: Exactly five.
Confessor: What kind of lies?
Penitent: Oh, just falsehoods.
Confessor: Falsehoods, huh? Well okay, lets have them.
Penitent: The first was that the earth is flat.
Confessor: (Jumping straight up out of his seat) Wait a second—it isn't flat?
Penitent:Not exactly.
Confessor: It sure as hell looks flat!
Penitent: Well some places it's almost flat. Very difficult for the naked private eye to tell the difference.
Confessor: Well, naked eyes are the only kind I got. So I guess that accounts for it. Go on.
Penitent: The second was that there is a God.
Confessor: (launching into a Jimmy Durante impersonation) Wait a minute! Wait a minute! You told no lie in that case, Daughter.
Penitent: You mean there is a god?
Confessor: Indubitably.
Penitent: And you can prove it?
Confessor: Just wait until you hear this proof. It's known as the poxological proof of the existence of god.
Penitent: I'm waiting,
Confessor:Is it not axiomatic that if there were not

a god, mankind would have had to have invented one?
Penitent: Sounds like something I heard somewhere.
Confessor: Probably in trigonometry. Anyway, has man invented god?
Penitent: Not as far as I know. There was an exhibition of the inventions of Thomas Edison at the Museum of Science and Industry last year and some of them looked pretty useful, although I didn't get to see the whole show because there was a power shortage and the lights went out, but I didn't see anything there that resembled a god and I'm pretty sure there would have been signs to god if any god were on exhibit there.
Confessor: There you have it. Quod erat demonstrandum est. There must be a god or else mankind would have invented him.
Penitent: That's pretty good.
Confessor: Just think with the mind of the church, my girl.
Penitent: The next lie was one that I told myself.
Confessor: You talk to yourself?
Penitent: Almost exclusively.
Confessor: It's an excellent way to assure yourself of a sympathetic audience. Well?
Penitent: Well, what?
Confessor: The lie! The lie that you told yourself?
Penitent: Oh yes. It was that I didn't care.
Confessor: That you didn't care what?
Penitent: That I didn't care if I lived or died.

Confessor: And you mean that's a lie?
Penitent: Yes , Father.
Confessor: How extraordinary!
Penitent: In fact I find it bothers me that I'm growing old.
Confessor: Richly amusing!
Penitent: And that there isn't any immortality.
Confessor: I guess it takes all kinds.
Penitent: Don't you care?
Confessor: Of course not.
Penitent: About anything?
Confessor: No. I just don't give a shit.
Penitent: You don't give a shit about your penitent?
Confessor: I don't give a shit about anyone, myself included.
Penitent: So you just don't give a fuck.
Confessor: Wait a second. Don't put words in my mouth. I definitely do give a fuck.
Penitent: When do you give a fuck?
Confessor: I give a fuck for your penance. On your feet!
Penitent: Mercy, mercy mercy…
Confessor: No Cannonball Adderley impression, please. Over to that bed. (A spotlight illuminates a plain but queen-size bed left center stage.)
Penitent: (Shrinking towards the bed) Be kind… be gentle . . .
Confessor: Off with your clothes! (And he strips her naked.) Onto your back!
(The confessor throws off his cassock leaving him-

self naked and tumescent. He dives upon the penitent and fucks her, in full view of the congregation, lengthily and in every orifice.)

After the penitent's final exhausted shriek of humiliation and delight, the lights go down on the stage and up in the auditorium, The congregation mills towards the lobby refreshment stand. Father Black beckons to Jimmy to join him in his dressing room.

The priest slips on slacks, a sweatshirt, and basketball shoes. He cracks a can of beer, offers one to Jimmy. Jimmy accepts and says, "How many times you do that?"

"It varies, I've picked up a few tricks along the way."

"Not a bad racket,"

"That's what I think. You never have to worry about where your next piece of ass is coming from. Saves on dates. Never seems to go out of style, although of course right now business is booming, what with the sorry excuse of a church that the priests of the undefrocked variety are putting forth for sale. Not fit for human consumption."

"I guess you're not with Elsa anymore."

"Oh no, we split up years ago. She's remarried. Couple of kids. She and I never had any."

"My mother wrote me that she heard you were teaching high school in Oklahoma."

"Joplin, Missouri, actually."

"No shit? Home of the Mickey Mantle Holiday Inn Motel?"

"Yeah. Big trophy case in the lobby."

"I know; I stayed there once. God, we could have gotten together and..."

"Well..."

"Yeah, you're right. I guess it would have been awkward."

"You know how hot-and-cold Elsa always ran."

"We were all in love with her and she drove us all nuts. Most beautiful girl in our class. But you'd be out one night with her and she'd be lovin' you up, and the next day she wouldn't spit at you. Not that any of us ever got that far with . . . "

"I know. It doesn't matter. I remember the time we were all coming back from New York and you and she were riding in the front seat of my Olds and she said she was tired and could she put her head on your lap and that night I saw you in line for confession?"

"She saw me too. She just laughed. These were grand trips to New York though. You taking us to the Sodality convention at Fordham but all of us staying at the Taft Hotel and going to doubleheaders at Yankee Stadium..."

"Mantle, Berra, Bauer, Whitey Ford..."

"I remember how awesome Herb Score was, shutting out the Yanks one evening..."

"His career ended by a linedrive off the bat of

Gil McDougald . . ."

"And I insisted we all go to Birdland and to the Copacabana . . ."

"Elsa loved you for it."

"We had to drag you to it."

"I was never the picture of sophistication. Still not, I'm afraid."

"I think the entire evening cost us about ten bucks each. Probably a hundred minimum today, but ten bucks was a splurge in 1957."

"I'm afraid the big apple is not on the itinerary of my little road show. Too tame. We'd be laughed out of town. You been back lately?"

"I rented a friend's apartment for three weeks three summers ago and took my kids back. It's still exciting, even with the changes. The Metropole is gone, and the Astor. Nothing is behind closed doors on 42nd Street."

"Would I like the new Yankee Stadium?"

"I don't think anyone who knew the old one would. You can't see the elevated running behind the outfield wall, and I bet you can't see in from it either."

"Johnny Puleo."

"Who'd he play for?"

"No: Johnny Puleo and his Harmonicats. I just remembered that they were on the bill at the Copa the night that we were there."

"You served mass for me at St. Patrick's Cathedral."

"I know. And each summer we made the obligatory visit to another cathedral: Radio City Music Hall."

"The Rockettes, the Corps de Ballet, always a good family film..."

"The last summer you got angry at all of us and gave us a lecture for, 'pairing off.'"

"It was a very confusing period for me. Also you were all trying to pair off with Elsa. I was determined that if I wasn't allowed into her pants none of you whippersnappers were going to find out what it was like there either."

"I think I understood that. I was quite the hypocrite back then myself. But I know that I rejoiced when I heard you'd quit the priesthood and run away with Elsa. Of course I was married and in graduate school by then."

"They were right, though, weren't they? Once a priest, always a priest, as you have just observed, hah, hah."

"What I just observed was one of the Carmina Burana."

"What?"

"Just some secular Latin hymns."

"You always had the literary bent."

"I wanted to be an athlete."

"God didn't give you sufficient God-given abilities, is how we would have put it then. But you worked at it as hard as anyone I'd ever known. Maybe that was what I liked about you. God knows there were plenty of things I didn't like. Do you remember the time I took you to New

York with my parents and you brought along your dumbells in your canvas bag and when the porter went to lift it his spine nearly fell out?"

"I'd been working out all summer. I couldn't see missing an entire week."

"You were the only one of the kids who always ate properly, even using a knife and fork on fried chicken. You'd been trained by your aunts in table etiquette as an essential of upward mobility. I hated you for your aunts. They always slipped me money on the side, and so I always felt I had to take you places."

"As I got older I realized what they'd been doing."

"And you helping me move to Canandaigua after the bishop transferred me as far as he could from Elsa, and all the way down and back you bawled your eyes out. Jesus, Jimmy, sometimes I thought sure you'd turn out gay."

"I can never figure it out either."

"Well, keep it under your hat. You make a statement like that nowadays and it won't be taken as a humble admission but as a flaunting of your alleged heterosexual superiority."

"I remember once when all us kids barged into your room at the Taft and you and Elsa were together on the bed."

"We were fully clothed.

"I know, but . . ."

"Okay, okay."

"Father?"

"Yes?"

"That summer you took us to New York with your parents?"

"Yes?"

"Do you remember after we returned and we were in your office with John Burton and you told him you were sorry that he hadn't been able to go because he had been your first choice?"

"I remember."

"Why did you say that in front of me?"

"I don't know."

"Didn't you know how hurt I'd be? How foolish I'd feel?"

"I'm sure I did."

"Then you wanted to hurt me?"

'I guess I did."

"I was just a child."

"I know."

"I loved you.'

"I didn't want you to. I think that's why I had to do it."

"Well, Father, that was only one bad day among many good ones: the meals at Schrafft's and Stouffer's and Child's . . . I thought they were gourmet extravaganzas in those days. And I remember that one morning I skipped Fordham . . ."

"We were always skipping Fordham, all of us,

even me, maybe me most of all. After registration day I think the closest any of us ever got to Fordham was Yankee Stadium or the Bronx Zoo."

"I know; well, anyway, this one morning I couldn't interest anyone in going to see what Greenwich Village was like, so I went myself. Of course there was nothing going on there in the morning, but I did see a basement theatre with less than a hundred seats that was advertising a play by someone named Ionesco. Then, the summer after my freshman year of college, I attended a cousin's wedding on Long Island, and afterwards my mother let me take a room for three nights at the Taft all by myself. I remember that I saw McLeish's J.B., and The West Side Story, which had just been given a second chance after a dismal opening run, and one night I went to the village and saw The Threepenny Opera, which was then the longest running play in the world. To me it was the height of avant-gardism. I also caught a late set at Birdland every night—sitting close enough to pick up one of Stan Kenton's drummer's drumsticks when it flew out of his hand—and I visited for the first time The Museum of Modern Art. I ate in the Stage Deli, although I didn't have much time for eating, and I went to a Yankee doubleheader and sat in the leftfield bleachers and was a little disgusted with all the naked-chested fat men and watched Rocky Colavito destroy the Yankees with his home run bat. Also I almost fell for a prostitution scam on

Times Square, the same one Claude Brown tells about in Manchild in the Promised Land where you end up waiting in a hotel room and the pimp has made off with your money."

"Was it then the scales tipped for you in favor of the literary over the athletic?"

"It wasn't exactly like Joyce's Epiphany on the Strand. There was more inevitability, less choice, to my vocation, and it was as much a question of what I was not good enough at as what I was, but, I suppose it was, well, a confirmation. A secular retreat, perhaps."

"Joyce, I know. I know he quit the church before you and I did."

"And with about as much success."

"I think there's hope for you. They haven't gotten you back in their clutches yet."

"Nor you."

"With me I think they'd say it's a matter of binary opposition. I'm the hell that gives definition to their heaven. The fallen that implies the saved."

"I didn't know you were into structuralism."

"I read it for my penance. I hope you go beyond it."

" I'll have to catch up with it first. I'm still most comfortable with Sartre and Camus."

Outside the theatre he finds a payphone and calls his girlfriend: "Laura?"

"Jimmy?"

"Are you sitting there being faithful to me?"

"Yes, but..."

"BUT???"

"But I've got a job."

"A job? Why a job?"

"No, it's why a duck? The job is because my money is gone and I have to pay the rent."

"When do you start?"

"I started this afternoon."

"Already? Without telling me?"

"Jimmy, I have no way to get in touch with you."

"What sort of job is it?"

"I'm a waitress at a country club."

"Oh my God, those rich guys will pay you to participate in orgies. Did you participate in an orgy this afternoon?"

"Jimmy, it's all old people. It's a very conservative place. It was mostly wives. I can't say that they don't treat the waitresses as human, but that's only because they think of themselves as divine. So they can afford to be tolerant of the merely human. I overheard one table of widows talking about sending their dogs to summer camp. One woman said her little Frou-Frou came back so refreshed: Another said the Samoans are buying up all the chickens in the market and that she's ordered her butcher to save some chickens back with a sign on them: "Not for the Samoans." It's disgusting how some of the veteran waitresses cater to them. And they were all ooohing and aaahing because Mitch Verna, the Pontiac dealer, was in the poker room."

"Poker room?" I thought you said it was all rich widows?"

"It practically is.'

"Did Mitch Verna try to get you to have sex with him?"

"Jimmy, nobody even noticed my existence,"

"Are you working any nights?"

"Once in a while. This Saturday night, I think, maybe."

"That's when they'll be putting the make on you."

"Jimmy, you're paranoid.'

"Never call me that."

"Okay, then, but you're wrong."

"We'll see. We'll see."

"When are you coming over?"

"How can I come over when you're working all the time?"

"Jimmy, I'm not working all the time. Just a few hours a week."

"I'll come over when I can."

He drives to the Art Theatre where the original uncut Caligula is playing. He cannot see at first inside the dark and crowded theatre, but he manages to feel his way to an empty seat on the aisle. It is not long before he finds himself erect. It is not much longer before he feels a hand on his erection. He allows the hand to gently stroke him towards satisfaction. Fortunately his muffled cry of pleasure is subsumed in the general hubbub of the Imperial Brothel. Afterwards his pupils are sufficiently dilated for him to see who has been making love to him:

"Laura!"

" Jimmy!"

"I thought you were sitting home being faithful to me."

"Well, uh, yes, of course I ordinarily would have been . . . but I had this intuition that you'd be coming to this movie. So I hurried over here and waited for you."

"How did you know where I'd be sitting?"

"I sat next to the only remaining empty seat in the house."

"But there are a lot of empty seats."

"That's because the movie just ended."

"You mean you rushed over here just to give me pleasure?"

"Yes, my love."

"You deserve an award . . . I should take you out for a fancy meal right here and now . . . and I would if I didn't have to run off . . . but I'll give you a rain check on it . . . I won't forget . . . Now you run home and lock yourself in your apartment."

He gets in his car and heads south on the

Pacific Coast Highway. In front of Don Jose's Motel he spots a naked hitchhiker. It is Laura's best friend, Clara. He stops for her, lets her into the car, and reaches a blanket from the back seat for her to wrap herself in. She does not seem injured. Clara is known for getting herself in predicaments.

"Well, what happened this time?"

"I met this man on a plane and he said he wanted to take pictures of me for a Swedish fashion magazine."

"Nude, of course."

"He said all the pictures in Swedish magazines are nude."

"Even in the fashion magazines?"

"I guess so"

"And a motel room makes a picturesque setting?"

"No, first we went to the woods and fields. He took a lot of rolls of film. He took pictures all day."

"Of what?"

"Of me."

"Of you standing there?

"Of me doing different things. Sometimes just normal things that you'd do outdoors. Sometimes trying to look attractive. Sometimes trying to look sexy."

"All by yourself?"

"Oh yes."

"And you felt comfortable?"

"Well, you know, I thought it might lead to a

glamorous career. And, yes, I think I did enjoy having pictures of my body taken. Except once, when he wanted me to masturbate for the camera, and I refused."

"So how did you get to the motel?"

"He invited me to his room for a drink. I felt like a drink."

"You didn't think he'd expect more than a drink?"

"I hoped he wouldn't. I was sure I'd be able to fight him off if necessary. And I was."

"He didn't hurt you?"

"No, I hurt him. That's why he locked me out without my clothes after I ran outside to get away from him."

Jimmy feels himself getting excited. He is tempted to come on to her himself. But who needs the aggravation? Who needs to end up as frustrated as the phony photographer back at the motel?

He lets her off in front of her place and tells her she can keep the old coat.

He stops at a phone and calls Laura. He wants her to have his version of running into Clara, just in case it gets modified along the way. Laura believes him. She trusts him in the most compromising situations and becomes insanely jealous over far-fetched fantasies. This is, he knows, because she does not in fact want to face the real possibility of infidelity on his part. She does not want to have to stop seeing him.

Tonight, though, she is upset over a call from

her mother. Her parents claim to be breaking up after forty years of marriage. Laura is outraged. How can they do this to her? Her parents' splitting up is an affront to herself, just as her older sister's going back to college is an obvious attempt to compete with her intellectually.

"How did your parents get so pissed at each other?"

"I don't know. Except that at one point my father apparently said to my mother, You've gotten so fucking fat that it disgusts me to look at you!"

"Is she pretty fat?"

"She's enormous."

"Probably she wanted him to fuck her when he wasn't feeling like it. Maybe she gave some hint that he wasn't the man he used to be, and so that was his way of striking back."

"That's possible."

"They'll get over it."

"My mother moved to the guest bedroom and packed her bags,"

"In a few days she'll start to unpack them. And sooner or later she'll move back to their bedroom."

"It just makes me so angry."

"It's their life."

"You mean it's none of my business. You mean I'm being self-centered again."

"I didn't say that."

"You meant it."

"Look, I've got to run."

He drives straight ahead till he comes to a bar

that he recognizes. He takes a stool at the horseshoe end of the counter next to a man he recognizes as Pat Stewart. Pat is perennially handsome in a graying, weatherbeaten way. Girls prefer him to his son, who sometimes bartends here. He's a winner at cards as well. He doesn't talk a lot and when he does, he doesn't say stupid things. Jimmy says, "What's happening?"

"Everybody's stinking. This morning was the Christmas party at the steam plant. The rum and bourbon were flowing before breakfast. I'm trying to catch up."

"Christmas? What year is this?"

"1974"

"Oh, yeah."

"Look at Frank Russell."

Jimmy looks over to where old Frank, enormous beerbelly preceding him, has wrapped his arms around the lovely-breasted barmaid and is performing a pantomine of doggy-style. Madge lets Frank get away with just about anything. Frank has been in love with every barmaid, and he loves each girl a little more than the last. He never actually gets anywhere with any of them, never really tries to . . . but he's copped more feels than any hundred other guys in town.

"Christmas Eve—his old lady's going to be pissed."

"He says he already warned her not to expect him. She's religious, so he told her to spend the whole night and day in church since that's the only place she's happy. And their kids are all grown, not to mention that Frank threw them all out of the house for telling their mother her religion was corrupt. She's something old fashioned like a Methodist, and the kids are all Jesus Freaks. I guess they want their mother to dress in rags and go around banging on a tambourine or something. Barry's the one that's going to be in trouble. You know Barry, in the black raincoat, teaches speech or something . . . I think he's always been a pretty straight-laced guy . . . and then the last couple of months he started dropping in here once in a while on the way home . . . and now he's in here all the goddamn time. His wife called the bar late the other night, and Thor started to call Barry to the phone . . . but Barry was giving him the cut-off sign, so Thor went back to the phone and said, 'No, I'm sorry, he isn't here anymore, I think he was here earlier but he went out with some of the guys to get a hamburg.' Then his wife starts bawling over the phone about how she worries about Barry and how he never used to leave her alone like this and how now that she needs him most, what with a small baby and everything, he's never around at all. And maybe he doesn't love her anymore, probably he's found some other woman, and on and on . . . and Thor had never even met the broad but he even starts to feel bad after a while, and God knows none of us has ever been as shitty to a wife as Thor was to both of his, but pretty soon he's reassuring her and telling her what a great guy Barry is and how he's always talking about how much he loves her and that as soon as he comes back in he's going to make sure he goes straight home. He hangs up the phone and goes down to the bar and tries to convince Barry that it's probably time he left, but Barry just says, 'That bitch, I'm never going home again, and Thor says, 'That's fine, Barry, but how far do you think you'll get on your ten-speed?' and Barry says, 'Okay, I'll have to go home tonight, but, just long enough to pack my bags and steal the car and I don't really know whether to laugh or cry, because just to look at Barry you can tell he's the most pussy-whipped soul ever to ride a bicycle up the PCH in the rain.

"So Barry's drunk and feeling brave and Thor gives up trying to talk him into going home and the next thing any of us know here come's Barry's wife in the front door with their little baby in her arms. Well, Barry was sitting right about here and she stormed in the door and right past him, probably because her eyes were still adjusting to the darkness, and Barry takes one look and dives down behind the bar trying to make himself invisible. His wife tears through the bar and into the back room and then she starts back toward us and I whisper to him, 'For Christ's sake, Barry, stand up and take it like a man, and I guess he does realize by that time that it's going to be a bit humiliating being caught by his wife crouching in a corner like a naughty little boy, because he stands up and says, 'Hi, honey . . . I kind of lost track of the time,' and she doesn't say a thing, just pinches him by the ear and leads him to his bicycle and he's kind of whimpering by now, and he rolls his bike outside, but she doesn't let go of his ear until he's on the bicycle, and then she follows him real slowly in the car all the way home . . .

"And tonight, Christmas Eve, he's back in the bar and drunk again."

"He looks happy."

"Doesn't he?"

Barry sees me looking down the bar at him and he waves happily and I wave back and Barry gets off his stool and journeys toward us. "You gentlemen mind if I join you here?"

"Our pleasure,"

"Merry Christmas!!! You know, it really is a merry Christmas in here,"

"Naturally."

"Not out there though. Not out in the world."

"No, not out in the world."

"I think that I'll just stay here. I think I just may spend my whole goddam vacation here."

"I'm afraid they may be closing early tonight. Probably in a couple of hours."

"0h. Oh dear. Well, then, I guess I'll just have to go home. That will make the queen bitch happy."

"Barry," Pat says gently, "your wife seemed like a very sweet young girl. Very pretty and she loves you very much. You sit around here calling her a bitch now and you'll only be feeling bad about it later."

"No I won't. I won't remember it later."

"Oh well, then," Pat says, "I guess I can't argue with that. Go ahead and call her whatever you want. In fact, I will too. I'll call her a bitch but I won't call her the queen bitch because I was married to the queen bitch. In fact, I was married to her a number of times."

"Turkey," Barry says.

"Turkey?"

"The bitch is cooking up a turkey."

"Isn't she starting it a little early'?"

"It's for tonight. We're celebrating Christmas tonight. We're having guests."

"Oh, Christ. What time?"

"I don't remember."

"Look, Barry, seriously, why don't you finish that one and hit the road."

"It's merry here. I like it here."

"We all like it here, but . . ."

"Pat," I say, "when you were married, were you ever late for any Christmas dinners."

"Jimmy, please be kind. I don't have Barry here's capacity for not remembering.'

"I just about missed a couple myself."

"I did miss one. I'm still ashamed to think about it, I picked up this gorgeous young thing at our office Christmas party and I just never went home. We were shacked up until after New Year. I tried to call home once or twice with some bizarre excuse in mind, but my wife had ripped the telephone out of the wall. She bought all the papers every morning, to read that I'd been killed on the highway. The marriage didn't last much longer after that."

"I've always hated Christmas. Always got sick at Christmas as a kid. California Christmases aren't so bad though. It was a revelation to me my first year out here when I discovered that everyone just drinks for two days straight — especially the Catholics."

"It do help a man to see it through."

"I wonder what you have to do around here these days to get a goddam beer.

Big Frank is about done dry-humping Madalyn by now, so I get her eye and she comes to our end of the bar and gives me a big kiss and says, "Please don't wish me Merry Christmas—I'm Jewish,"

"We know," Pat says; "Gentiles don't have tits like that."

"Is that all you ever think about?"

"I'm sorry, Madalyn. I forget you don't like to be considered a sex object. It might be easier for me to remember it, though, if you'd ever wear a bra beneath your see-through blouses."

"Do you really want me to?"

"As a matter of fact, what I really want you to do is to take the damn blouse off altogether."

"When I feel like taking it off, I take it off."

"I hear you felt like taking it off down at the

Ancient Mariner last night. I hear that you took all your clothes off."

"You hear wrong; I had a body stocking on."

"We'll settle for that."

"I don't have one on today."

"Our tough luck. What is this anyway, you going around taking off your clothes for a bunch of strangers. Aren't we good enough in here for you?"

"Your time will come."

"I'm getting old."

"Don't call attention to the obvious."

"Hey, shit, let's not be mean."

"I'm sorry. I guess I'm just worn out from putting up with Frank all afternoon."

"He loves you, Madge."

"I love him too. Today was just a little longer than usual. And drunker. I went over to the steam plant with those guys this morning."

"Well, what are the chances of me getting a drink myself before 1999?"

"I'm sorry, Jimmy. A small one?"

"Don't we have anything back there besides beer?"

"I think there's still some rum."

"I'll have a rum-and-coke. Plenty of coke. My stomach can't take the straight stuff anymore."

Madalyn goes to get the surreptitious rum from behind the bar, and Barry says to him, wide-eyed with incredulity, 'Do you think there's any chance she'll really take her clothes off?"

"She just might!"

"Really?

"She'll take them off," Pat says.

Madalyn returns with Jimmy's drink and Pat says, "Come on, Madge, a little Chanukkah present for your faithful admirers."

"Pat, I don't really feel like it."

"You'll never feel like it until you do it. You've just got a mental block against it,"

"I don't have any mental blocks about anything. It's my body and I do what I want with it."

"You've got us all aroused already."

"You must be easily aroused."

"We are. Come on, sweetheart, show us Santa Clause can be a woman."

"Ohhhh . . . fuck fuck fuck there!"

With one quick gesture she lifts the lightweight blouse off over her head and stands there naked from the waist up.

At twenty-eight, Madalyn has just the slightest tummy and she does have very beautiful breasts, large and sloping outward like a classic, cushioned ski run.

Frankly, Jimmy is speechless. Next to him he hears Barry exhale, "Gaaaa — daaaaaam!"

Jimmy has to admit that he is not used to looking at naked women in public places. He wants to look and still he finds himself involuntarily turning his eyes away. He's embarrassed to get caught staring.

While Madalyn is standing there, resigned,

arms at her side, Pat inconspicuously slips the blouse from her hands. When she reaches for it, he draws it out of her reach. "Please, Pat," she says.

"You said you were going to take off all your clothes."

"I never said any such thing."

"You don't want to cop out on your friends."

"Pat, give me back my blouse."

She is self-conscious now, tries to shield her breasts from view with her arms.

"Just take the rest off and then I'll let you have the blouse back."

"I don't want to take the rest off. I want my blouse back."

"It will only take a second."

There is tension in the air now. Jimmy is beginning to wonder how much exactly old Pat has in mind.

"Please, please . . . someone may come in."

"We'll lock the door. Give us the key."

Now Jimmy is pretty sure exactly what Pat has in mind. There are tears in Madalyn's eyes.

As quietly as possible, Jimmy says, "Give her her blouse, Pat."

Pat looks at Jimmy as if he has betrayed a trust.

"Pat, give her the blouse."

He does. She slips immediately into it.

"Madalyn, let me have another rum-and-coke. And one for Pat and one for Barry."

"The rum's all gone, Jimmy," she says, choking

a little.

"I'll make a run for some," Jimmy says.

When Jimmy returns from the liquor store, which is only two blocks away, Pat is gone. Madalyn is weeping openly now.

"What happened?"

"He . . . offered me fifty dollars to take my clothes off."

"It's a lot of money to be tossing around."

"I told him that was prostitution"

"I suppose. . ."

"I feel so rotten, Jimmy."

"So does he."

"I feel unclean."

"And he feels old."

"He is old."

"If you think in those terms."

"Oh, Jimmy, I'm just glad it's over. I should never have let it get started."

"Let's just shine it on, Madalyn. It's just a thing that started out good and went bad."

"What was good about it?"

"What was good about it was your body. My jaw must have dropped a foot. Barry just about dislocated his."

"I did,"Barry insists. "It was really wonderful! I couldn't believe my eyes. Do you think that maybe some other time again you might. . ."

"Ohhhhhhh, Jimmmmmmmmmmy. . ."

"Barry, for Christ's sake. . ."

"I'm sorry, I'm sorry."

"Look, Madalyn," I say, trying painstakingly to get it right; "the tease. . . the disrobing , the conquest, these things are always going to be a part of sex. So much of sex is in the head that. . ."

"Not for my generation," she says. "For Pat Stewart's generation, yes. And maybe for yours, although I can't really believe that you believe all that, but not for mine."

"You're sure?"

"We make love because it's the natural thing to do. We don't need all that worn-out psychic paraphernalia to make it exciting. It's fun in itself."

"It is?"

"Sure. You know that, Jimmy."

"No, I'm not sure I do. How about the men of your so-called generation? Are you sure that you can speak for them?"

"I'm sure. And it's not too late for anyone. Your friend, Jack Heinz, for instance. He's become a beautiful person. Two years ago he was a prick."

"I didn't know you were still seeing him."

"I'm not. I couldn't take his going home to a wife and kids."

"He's left them."

"He'll go back."

"Yeah, I suppose so."

"But I wish that Pat could leam a few things from him, And you, if you're serious. And Chaz.

Jack Heinz has got his head straight!"

"Well, then, I'm glad for him. But I'm afraid I'm not convinced. I'm afraid my mentor, the good Marquis, left his mark upon me at an impressionable age,"

"Oh, Jimmy, that's a lot of bullshit. I'm hereby making you an honorary member of the younger generation."

"Do you think I could get away with dual citizenship?"

He finishes his beer and steps out into a summer's day. The car he approaches is the brown Dodge that his father bought, second-hand, in 1950. His parents are in the front seat. "Hurry up," they say, and gesture him towards the back seat. "You're supposed to be at Camp Stella Maris for check-in before three."

He has been waiting all year for this, his first week of summer camp. He has daydreamed through dull classes, imprecise visions of athletic prowess and living-in-nature. It has never occurred to him that he will miss his parents. Sure, there were times when he was little that he begged his aunts or neighbors to take him home, and sure, except for a few trips to the mountains with his aunts, he has not, in recent years, been away from home for any length of time, and yes, he was at one time something of a Mama's Boy, what with his father away at war for the first four years of his life, and yes, there was that traumatic time that his mother went away in the taxi for her goiter operation and the babysitter made the mistake of letting him watch her departure from the window, precipitating a nearly uncontrollable fit of tears, and yes, his aunts did make the mistake of letting him in his mother's room before she had come out of the anaesthetic, the iodine blood-red on her throat, and it is true that he cried the first day of kindergarten and that on certain mornings in first grade he disrupted the family by refusing to go to school until his father wisely and firmly ended that by hauling him off to his bed and leaving orders that he would not be allowed to go to school that day but no, it has in all truth never occurred to him that he will once again be gripped by the irrational paralysis of homesickness.

But even now, riding in the car towards Lake Conesus, he feels it building in his gut. At the Camp itself, the bustle of registration and a few familiar faces and the promise of non-stop activities raise his heart somewhat, but as his parents go off down the hill, the tears take hold of him and he rushes after them, begging, "I don't want to stay; take me home with you; don't leave me here."

They tell him he is going to be fine, that as soon as they're out of sight he'll be having a great time and happy that he didn't follow his initial feelings.

He knows this is not true; He knows he will be miserable. He knows that he has never enjoyed being stranded among strangers; He knows the occasional pleasures of the week will not outweigh its basic misery.

But how can he convey this to them? They have no way of knowing how deeply, kinesthetically unhappy he is. They are certain they are doing what is best for him.

His mother says "Here comes one of your counselors. It's time for you to go with the others to your cabin. You don't want to have your counselor see you crying."

Of course the counselor is going to be able to tell from his wretched eyes that he's been crying but his mother's warning is enough to stem the tears. She and his father hurry off down the hill, as the young male counselor, a seminarian, leads Jimmy off to Grizzly Cabin, distracting him with a recitation of the evening's schedule.

He is all right, then, through the softball game, at which he is the winning-pitcher, and through the busy dinner. A sadness comes over him at the campfire—are not all campfires inherently melancholy? After lights out it seems he will be unable to hold back from sobbing--until a fortunate pillow fight breaks out. By the time an ostensibly strict counselor returns to end the fun with threats of phonecalls to parents, he is sufficiently exhausted to fall asleep.

He is too rushed at taps—through calisthenics, Mass, breakfast, and inspection—to have time for sorrow. And he tears up the court at the morning's basketball game. But there is free time for arts or crafts just before lunch where he finds himself not wanting to do anything but write his folks a letter asking them to come for him. He resolves to write such a letter during rest hour after lunch.

Rest hour turns out to be fun, though, with the counselor telling stories and teaching them riddles. He eats the allotted candy bar and writes no letters.

He has never liked the water, although he is not a bad swimmer. He doesn't mind the lessons, which make the time pass, but he hates the free swim, which all the others love. He is cold and bored and frightened of the rough house and he slows the passage of the minutes by dwelling on them. Even the watched pot does, however, eventually boil.

He has another spectacular outing at baseball. Without trying to, just in the nature of his enjoyment of the competition, he is earning recognition and respect from the counselors and the other campers. He is beginning to hear his name on other people's lips.

The evening's meal is awful—some kind of chicken and gravy—but the evening ration of one soft drink—he chooses a birch beer—helps to cleanse his palate, And this campfire turns out to be fun with stories of the H-Man (the letter burned on his chest by the window bars that kept him from rescuing his family from the burning farmhouse) and the legendary Hook-Arm. He will not sit upon the open toilets—he has never seen such a thing in his life—until after everyone else is in bed. Strolling to the latrine building, he half-listens for the mad cry of the H-Man. He hasn't believed the stories, of course, but he wants to think, as all boys do, Wendy's most famously, that he inhabits a world of danger and excitement.

Tuesday morning he experiences intimations of depression half-way through the Mass. They ease over breakfast, but when he fails in mid-morning to fashion anything resembling a proper piece of jewelry for his mother in the craft-shop, he finds himself sitting under a tree, weeping. A counselor discovers him there, and unable to bring him out of it, takes him to the camp nurse, a kindly, maternal nun. Just being with her makes him feel better, but it is only when she promises to call his parents that he returns to the camp regimen and, after lunch, is called aside and assured by his cabin counselor that his parents, who had originally thought it not a good idea to attend the Wednesday evening reception for parents, will indeed be driving up.

He is fine then, hurling himself into the basketball and baseball and races and wrestling and boxing and games of tag, and tolerating the swimming and crafts and unfamiliar recipes and the horrible toilets and the corny talent-show skits.

When it comes time for his parents to arrive, he is of course embarrassed to have summoned them. He is fine now. They were right. His homesickness was just a thing he had had to get over. He talks animatedly with them, introduces them to new friends, blushes as a counselor extols his athletic successes. It is only near the end of the showing of the evening movie, The Song of Bernadette, that he finds, incredibly, the intolerable tropism returning.

"You'd better go on now to your campfire," his mother says. "You'll get in trouble if you're late,"

"Let me go home with you, he says, "Please."

"That wouldn't be good for you," his mother says. And his father says, "You'll be wanting to come for the two-week session next summer and if we let you come home now how will we be able to put down the deposit with any confidence?"

"It's only two more days," his mother says. "We'll be here for you on Saturday. Everyone says that Thursday and Friday are the most fun. You want to compete for your side in the camp Olympics, don't you?'

He does want to. He's been looking forward to it.

A group of kids from his cabin go by and call for him. They look at him just a little funny. He is a better athlete than any of them. He says, "I'll see you Saturday," and heads for the campfire, avoiding any groups of kids.

On Thursday the entire camp is divided into two sides, the blues and the golds.Competitions are held in everything imaginable. Jimmy leads the gold basketball team to an easy win and pitches the softball team to a close victory in which he also hits a home run. He is an important grip on the winning tug-of-war team. He is among the point-winning finalists in the long-run and the softball throw.

Thursday night is the carnival, with penny candies as prizes in the midway games, and Friday is the War of the Woods—a march through scorched cornfields with the cry of the H-Man echoing from over the hills, followed by a military encounter with balls of wet newsprint as weapons. The Blues win that one.

At the Friday night awards banquet, Jimmy wins Best Basketball Player. He is so sure that he deserves Best Baseball Player as well that he is already beginning to rise when he realizes the name being read out is that of his first-baseman, little Tommie Quinlan. It is Jimmy's first experience of divvying up the glory. It strikes him as basically unfair, but it is soon put out of his mind by the announcement of his having been voted Best Camper. How could he, he asks himself, have been Best Camper, when he has not even wanted to be there and he's caused so much trouble and he's behaved like such a baby? He accepts the award anyway, and the congratulations, and figures he must have won it for sticking it out.

That should be the end of it. Ending on a winning note. But for some reason that he will never fathom, his parents do not pick him up early on Saturday morning. They are not even among the late arrivals. They are among the absolute last, at least an hour after every other kid and many of the counselors have gone home. Jimmy sits an a hill and tries to keep from crying and accepts the combined congratulations and consolations of the counselors remaining and watches the lake road for signs of the brown Dodge.

And once again, the pot, though watched, does eventually boil. And he forgives them everything in his joy at seeing them and talks a gold streak all the way home,

But why in the world had they had to be so late? Thirty years later, a night person himself, he will figure they had no doubt taken advantage of their last night of freedom to go out with friends and had arisen late and probably hungover. None of his own kids will grow up infected with that helpless homesickness, but he still vows to never leave them sitting waiting.

He marries when he is twenty and goes off to graduate school. He visits his mother in the summer of 1964. In 1965 he splits up with his first wife and three children and remarries. His mother just about disowns him. She gets over that, but twenty years later he has still not gone back again to see her, although they do talk on the phone, nor is she invited to visit him.

He tries to leave his first wife twice before succeeding, but returns both times. The first time is a Saturday morning and their good friends and neighbors upstairs are crying as he packs his car and pulls out of the driveway. But it is a depressing Saturday morning in Alhambra, California, with nothing to distract him, so an hour later he drives back in and unpacks the car.

The second time he thinks he is in love with this beautiful black girl and that she is in love with him. It is only after he's moved out that he learns his love is not reciprocated. Two days later he returns.

The third time, when he has another woman to live with, he is able to move out for good.

And four years later, when he has yet another woman to move in with, he once again moves out of marriage.

On trips to Europe, if alone, he grows literally sick with homesickness. He drinks to keep himself from flying home early. He drinks so much he has sometimes to be helped onto the return flight.

In his forties Jimmy's great fear is that, left alone without a family or at least a woman, he will be destroyed by this paralyzing homesickness.

His cabin counselor, who used to love to wrestle with the campers, will grow up to be a priest in

Jimmy's parish. He will wrestle with Jimmy, who is in high school then. And Father Black will say to Jimmy, "Doesn't Father So-and-So seem just a bit effeminate to you?" He doesn't, but then again Jimmy is very naive. Years later he will wonder if Father So-and-So was using those wrestling matches to get his rocks off. Maybe, since he had usually made sure that they were private. But Jimmy will search his mind without recollecting a single obviously sexual touch. At the time his main suspicion had been that Father So-and-So was using the wrestling for an excuse to talk to him about a possible vocation.

And thirty years later he would still be trying to write about Camp Stella Maris. As a young writer, he would try to impose a plot on it, not one of triumph over adversity, because he never felt he had triumphed, but rather silly romantic encounters with beautiful women in the hills beyond the cabins under a July moon. Bronte stuff, but without the instinct for the genre. And he would always give up.

That was why, as he would tell his students, there were no literary prodigies—because you not only had to have something to write about but you had to learn how to write about it. Experience and the coming to grips with experience, the understanding of it, at least on an intuitive level, and finally the intuition of how to use your life as literature. Prodigies, that is, in the sense of Mozart writing symphonies at six. There was nothing prodigious about Rimbaud reversing the laws of imagery in his late teens or schoolgirl Francoise Sagan dealing with older men who left their wives for girls her age.

He would come to realize that his lifelong homesickness had its benefits, preventing him, for instance, from ever seriously considering the military as a career. Camp Stella Maris was to be as close as he would ever let himself come to basic training.

And when he would eventually come to write of the Camp, he would still feel that there was one ingredient missing—that pinch of romance on the heath. It was probably what had made him think he wanted to go to camp in the first place. It was what he had thought he had always wanted to write about. Of course for years it was unthinkable that he should write about his deepest insecurities. Still, at moments on camping trips with a wife and kids, when he would slip from the tent to take a piss beneath Wyoming stars, he would recapture a shiver of the mysterious delight that he had hoped at first to find at Camp and later to impose on his imaginative version of it. He'd return to sit on a picnic bench a while, wondering what romance beyond that of ostensibly illicit love was left to him. But it was cold out and his back was stiff. He'd take a swig of Seven Crown and go back to the tent.

Jimmy is so happy to be back with his mom and dad that he swears to himself that he will never leave their presence again. But bounding from the brown Dodge to their apartment building, he notices kids playing football at the playground across the street. "Is it all right if I go play for a while?"

"Of course. Just come right home when I call you for dinner."

He starts across the street, but there, at a diagonal from the brown Dodge, he recognizes his own white Toyota station wagon. He extracts the key from his pocket, hops in behind the wheel, and drives straight to a pay phone. He dials his girlfriend's number. A recorded message breaks in to inform him that the number has been disconnected. He tries again. Same message.

He drives to the apartment. There is a note on the door. It says, "I've decided to go to the University of the Northwest and get my doctorate in Comparative Misery. Here's my number in the graduate dorm." He drives to another pay phone and calls the long distance number collect.

"Jimmy, I was hoping you'd call!"

"I'm sorry I didn't have enough change in my pocket to. . ."

"That doesn't matter. I just started classes today and I have the most wonderful professor of Modern European Misery. I just love him, He's a Scandinavian and there are only three of us in the class, and he's just so. . ."

"You what him?"

"His mind. Isn't it all right to love a Great Mind?"

"My mind is what you always said attracted you to me. And mine isn't even very good, not to mention my body, although a little football will get that back in shape."

"Oh, Jimmy, don't spoil my excitement."

"When are you coming back?'

"Soon. Three months at the longest."

"But you won't have your apartment then."

"No, you'll have to find someplace else for us to be together."

"Why did you have to go to a school so far away?"

"I was jealous of you and your wife."

"I told you that you were exaggerating."

"I couldn't get thoughts of the two of you making love out of my mind."

"But you can get rid of those thoughts up there?"

"It's easier,"

"And then you have your Scandinavian misery teacher to occupy your thoughts."

"Jimmy."

"Okay."

"The time will pass quickly. Really."

"Okay."

Somehow he doesn't feel as if he has a girlfriend anymore.

He realizes that the bottom has just fallen out of the shopping bag in which he carries himself around.

He takes another dime from his pocket and calls a thoroughly westernized oriental girl of his acquaintance: "Jimmy?"

"How could you have known it was me? I haven't called you in months."

"That's how I knew it was you. I was sitting here thinkin, That asshole hasn't called me in months. I'm just about due for a call from that sonofabitch. I bet he's going to suggest we 'get together,'"

"Well, as a matter of fact. . ."

"Unh-unh, Charlie. I don't take well to rejection.'

"I didn't exactly reject you."

"No, you just plain and simple dumped me. And dumped on me. Humiliated me in front of my friends. Told me I was a manipulator and a prick-tease and spoiled and too used to always getting my own way."

"You are."

"Then why are you calling me?"'

"I guess I thought maybe you'd improved

your character."

"Bullshit. How's your girlfriend?"

"Well, actually . . ."

"She dumped you, didn't she? I knew it. Good for her."

"I guess I can take it that you're not interested in us, uh. . ."

"Getting it on? Isn't that your favorite way of putting it?"

"It's one of my favorites."

"Your back still giving you trouble?"

"God, yes."

"Would it feel good if we found a room somewhere and before we did anything else I just walked on your back with my bare feet for about an hour?"

"That would be great."

"Dream on, Casanova. Give me a call again six months from now. Maybe my character will have improved by then."

He calls home: "Everything okay?*

"You're not here, are you?"

"No, I'm not there. I'm here."

"Then everything is wonderful. There's a letter for you though. It's from your oldest daughter. Do you want me to read it to you?"

"Oh, I suppose I should come home and pick it

up. It wouldn't be right for a third person to open a letter to a man from his daughter."

"I already opened it,"

"Oh."

"So I'll just read it to you and then there will be no need for you to come home."

"I guess you might as well."

"Dear Jimmy. . . Well, I'll just summarize the parts about herself. She's doing well in school and she's seen some good movies and she's read some good books and she has some good friends. . . Here, here's the interesting part: 'Also, in my health sciences class we've been studying alcoholism and I hope you won't be offended, and I really respect many things about you, and I find it very hard to say this, but because I love you so much and I hate to see you destroying your health and I think you may even be going a little bit nutsy-cuckoo, I feel I have to tell you that I've decided you're an alcoholic. Love, Marta. P.S. The rest of the family and all my friends and everyone else I've discussed this with, including the members of my health sciences class and the professor, all agree that I'm right."

"How nice of her to find time to write in the midst of all her school activities."

"I thought it would raise your spirits. You've seemed a little depressed lately."

"Actually, in comparison with today, I've been on a natural high."

"Well, I suppose you'll want to go drink yourself into oblivion now."

"To tell you the truth, I was thinking about coming home and putting the kids to bed and maybe you and I could roll around on a mattress for a while."

"No, thanks."

"Oh. Okay. Any particular reason?"

"I can give you one if you want one: crocheting, the garden, my favorite soap opera, too much of a good thing. . ."

"It's been three years."

"Three wonderful years."

"Not since we've been together. It's been fifteen wonderful years since we've been together. It's been three years since we did the dirty last."

"Three wonderful years. But, incidentally, hasn't it also been one wonderful year since the last time you asked?"

"That's about right."

"So I can assume that you've been banging someone else for at least a year?'

"Now, now let's not jump to any hasty conclusions."

"And I can deduce that whoever you have been sticking it into has most likely just told you to get fucked somewhere else."

"Now that is not exactly necessarily precisely unequivocally. . ."

Click.

"Hello?"

"Teri?"

"Yes."

"This is Jimmy Abbey. Do you remember me?'

"Of course."

"How long has it been?"

"Ten years. Maybe twelve."

"Are you still nineteen-years-old?"

"Yes."

"How sweet of you! You've been sitting there waiting for me to call again for twelve long years."

"Some were longer than others. But yes, basically."

"No other men? Not even a kiss?"

"No one else."

"What about your boyfriend in the wheel chair who broke his neck diving into the surf. The one that just before that had dumped you for cute little Zelda Fitzgerald, but who decided after he was paralyzed for life and you kept coming to see him and she never did that she was a fickle little bitch and that it had been a mistake for him to dump you on her behalf? I always figured you were jacking him off."

"I deny it."

"Not even to make up to him for the time you and all your friends were fooling around after dark at Recreation Park, and when the cops arrived everyone made a mad dash for the car, but, clearing a curb, you dumped him out of the wheelchair on his face?"

"Negative."

"You don't prefer him to me on the Michael Furie--Jake Barnes theory that the best lover is one who not only can't have you but can't have anyone else either?"

"I swear not,"

"What about your boss at the hamburger stand? Is he still trying to get you into the meat freezer with him? Is he still making constant allusions to your cute legs and butt?'

"Yes, but it doesn't do him any good. If I ever did get into the freezer with him I'm sure the blood would drain from more than his face. He's such a bore that most of the girls have quit their jobs and he's in danger of losing his for not being able to keep any employees."

"You do realize that your butt is not quite as cute since you've been on birth control pills?"

"I know, I know, when I look at myself after a shower I want to cry. But would you rather that I stopped taking them?"

"No, not yet, Although I have to admit that there was something exciting about the old pregnancy roulette we used to play back in those days when you were rooming with your sister and she'd be at work in the afternoons and I'd come over after working out with the weights and showering and picking up a bottle of cheap champagne on the way. And we'd sit around the kitchen getting high on the bubbly, and when I'd suggest we go to bed, you'd say no, we'd better not until you had a chance to do something about birth control, but we'd drink some more and I'd start playing around with you and I'd prop you up on my lap and eventually I'd get you in on your bed anyway—or preferably on your sister's—and I'd be telling you how careful I was going to be, but of course I'd always come in you anyway, and we'd usually have time to fuck twice before the clock-radio that we'd set would herald your sister's arrival. What exquisitely pleasurable summer afternoons."

"Then the crotchety old fuck next door blew the whistle to my sister. I had parked five minutes in front of his garage once, and he took the opportunity to avenge himself on me. I had just sat down to dinner with the family one Sunday afternoon when my sister asked, 'By the way . . . Teri, who's the husky guy with the beard who stops by with a bottle of wine nearly every afternoon?"

"Do you think she had a suspicion who it was?"

"She may have. She'd had a crush on you at one time."

"I wish she'd shown it. I always wanted to fuck her, and I really came onto her once when we were drinking beer, but she seemed committed to the guy she was engaged to. She thought she could have me as a platonic friend. I explained to her, as I have to so many women, that I have enough male friends with whom I have much more in common than I have with women, and that I have a few women friends, such as ex-wives, that one develops incidentally along the way, and that I was not in the market for any more female friends. For one thing, how can you bitch to women about the way women are? Mostly I just don't like them to think they can have their cake without eating it too. I assume you knew I'd wanted to fuck your older sister."

"I suspected it."

"Your younger sister too. Do you think you could arrange for me to go to bed with the three of you sometime?"

"It wouldn't be easy. And I'd rather not."

"But you would do it for me, wouldn't you?"

"Yes."

"Then do your best. Did that guy ever ask you out again who invited you to a party at the yacht club and when he picked you up and you weren't dressed fancy enough said, 'Why don't we just go to a movie tonight, and some other time, when you're more dressed for the occasion, we'll go over to the club?'"

"He called once, but I wouldn't go to the phone."

"What about Bob?"

"Which Bob?"

"Oh yeah, I remember, all of your boyfriends except me were named Bob. I was forced to devise epithets for them to keep them straight: Burger-Bob, Frat-Bob, Yacht-Bob, Cannabis-Bob. No, I mean Pussy-Bob, the regular boyfriend that you'd been going with for years without even being decent to him, let alone letting him have a little."

"Jimmy, he's so awful. I can't help but tell him ever and over what an asshole he is. He takes me to the worst restaurants and the worst movies, He brings me chocolate bunnies. He invited me to his place for his own special spaghetti. Not even stroganoff, for Christ's sake. He served Gallo Hearty Burgundy, no doubt because he'd believed the commercials that it beat all those French wines in blind tastings, and he even decanted it at the table. I only kept my sanity by trying to guess at which point in the evening he would make his move. In point of fact it came just after he had cleared from the table my untouched slice of Sarah Lee cherry pie. I used the pass as an excuse for rushing home in a huff."

"Why do you go out with him?'

"So my parents won't ask me why I don't go out at all. It wouldn't be so bad if he wouldn't call or come by every night. Even when he can tell I'm trying desperately to cram for an exam, he hangs around, just shooting the shit. What a nerd!"

"We've had some good times."

"I'm glad you seduced me."

"Seduced you? Teri, the first time I gave you a ride home, you pulled your pants down and mine and sat on my dick."

"I was hot."

"I was complimented. But I was scared shitless

the time your father stalked into the bar and hauled your ass home. I remeber coming out of the head and here is this white-haired guy standing over you reading you the riot act. You snapped out of there as if you were a rubber band. I thought both our asses were grass. I settled down to getting stinking drunk and I even submitted to a blow-job from a promiscuous woman whom I would never have had anything to do with had I not been trying to blank my mind. As she was getting out of my car, she discovered your school books. The next morning I called a cop-friend of mine and we drove out to the hamburg joint to return the schoolbooks. He wanted to see if you were obviously underage in appearance. He took one look and said, "You never saw her consume a drop." But you weren't even nonplussed. When I asked you if there was any chance your father would make any legal problem, you said, 'Over drinking? Oh no, he's Irish, he thinks everyone should drink. It's only sex that he objects to.' And when I asked you how he'd known how to find you, you said you'd called home and left a message that you were going drinking with one of your teachers."

"I learned my lesson. But we did have good times, didn't we? I mean that first time that we went to the track and won a lot and you would have won the exacta if you'd bet it 5-8, like I told you, instead of 8-5, as you insisted. And the times we'd be sitting in the bar having a beer and you'd get rubbing my back or my thigh and then you'd say, "What the fuck; what's a Visa card for? Let's go to a motel.' Or when we'd just park in your car down by the oil wells and I'd go down on you while you rammed your hand as far as it would go up inside me . . ."

"You were vaginal to a fault."

"What?"

"I thought I'd break my wrist. Also your mouth was too large,"

"I thought a large mouth was an advantage."

"It can be, but in your case something was wrong, You gave a lot of head, but you didn't give much good head. On the other hand, or from the other end, I did enjoy pushing my way through your kinky pubic hair."

"I'm sorry about the second time we went to the track. I was just drunk and pre-menstrual. I knew I was talking too much but I just couldn't shut the motor off. I don't know why I went on so about whether to change my major to ceramics and how I wanted to kill myself . . ."

"It was the beginning of the end. Crazy women scare me off. So do women who try to manipulate me with threats to themselves"

"I won't do it again. I promise. Look, could we get together someplace this evening?"

"Well, there's a Lakers-Celtics game I want to watch . . ."

"We can watch it together."

"And I don't want to kill the entire

evening ."

"You can drop me back here any time you want."

"Okay, meet me at the usual place by the pizza joint in half an hour."

He picks her up at the corner, stops at a liquor store for some rum and cokes, drives to a dirt-cheap motel on Signal Hill. They pour down a couple of drinks, fuck, and turn on the t.v. They watch the first quarter of the game, her pretty much keeping her mouth shut, and then he turns off the t.v. and fucks her again, not wasting any time so as to be able to catch the end of the first half. They fuck again at half-time and then he figures, fine, great, so much for the sex, now we can just settle in with a couple more drinks and enjoy the second half.

Pretty soon she is running off at the mouth again. He realizes she is drunk. He has no sympathy for this. She has done enough drinking in her perpetually young life to have learned how to handle it, to have found her limit.

When she starts complaining about cramps, he pays her little attention.

When she rolls off the bed and lands heavily on the floor, he pays her no attention. Not until the Lakers call a time-out. Then he gives her a Maalox.

A few minutes later she is wretching in the

bathroom. The score is tied and there are only a few minutes left in the game.

When she comes out she says she is feeling a lot better. He tells her she had better start getting dressed. She gets her socks on, and then the stomach pains come back and she rolls off the bed with a thud again.

The big Celtic forward throws up a desperation jumper, which goes in, as they always seem to, and they are in overtime. He has not intended to stay this long.

He asks her if she is going to be okay, and she says yes. She shoves one tit into her bra and then falls back in a lump on the threadbare carpet.

When the Lakers lose in double-overtime he is really pissed. He rather roughly helps her dress and all-but-carries her to the car. Fifty yards from her house he stops the car and gets her pointed in the right direction, still clutching her gut and moaning. He watches her ring the doorbell, but he doesn't stick around for the opening of the door.

Slug it, "Finis for Teri." He won't be calling her again.

He decides to stop home anyway. His wife greets him with surprising cordiality. Immediately he concludes she must want something. Must need something. Something must have gone wrong for her. She must need his support against someone else.

Sure enough she starts right in with, "Can you imagine what that dumb bitch Megeen in the front apartment did last night? She left her new car parked behind mine so I couldn't get out to go to work and take the kids to school this morning. And I didn't know whose car it was so I had to wake up the manager first to find out and then I woke up Megeen and told her not to ever park behind me again, and she yelled, 'Don't you scream at me,' but she moved her car, and I had made up my mind just to call the police the next time and have her car towed away, but the manager not only told me she was moving back to the Mid-West, but guess who it looks like the new manager is going to be?"

"Oh no."

"Oh yes. Megeen. I can't believe it. Why would the landlord do that?"

"He probably just wanted to do a favor."

"No, Daddy," chirps in their five-year-old, who has been absorbing the whole conversation, "he didn't do us a favor."

"I meant a favor for Megeen. Lower her rent a little."

"Well, if that idiot is going to be manager, I'm not paying any rent."

Jimmy moves back out of his daughter's sight and signals, "Little ears sometimes tell tales" and to his chagrin, his wife spins on their daughter and commands, "I don't want to hear a word of this repeated, Do you understand"

Now their daughter is sobbing and Jimmy says, "I didn't mean to get her yelled at. I meant perhaps we should wait to discuss it until sometime when we wouldn't be putting the kids in the position of having to keep secrets."

"All right," his wife snaps, "I want you kids both into the bathroom and then I'll read you a story in bed and then we're going to sleep." And she slams the bedroom door on her husband.

He goes to the refrigerator and takes out a bottle of wine and pours himself one. He sips it until he hears the bathroom door open. Then he enters the bedroom and says, "Come on, you two, and give me a hug and kiss before bed," and they are doing so, while he tells them he loves them, even as their mother is trying to drown him out with, "Will you children please come here like I asked you to?"

"Jesus Christ," he mutters. "Go ahead, you guys,"

The bedroom door comes firmly shut again in his face.

He refills his glass with wine and goes to sit by the typewriter. He picks up the fragment of a manuscript he had been working on a while ago . . . how long ago. . .seems like weeks ago . . . months ago, years ago. . .

He begins to read it . . .

The Longest Jet Lag:

A Novel by Jimmy Abbey

The longest jet lag started when he returned from the extended assignment in Europe. Nothing seemed changed the evening she and his infant daughter met him at the airport. She was restrained towards him, but she had been before he left as well. As he had been towards her. He had changed overseas, had come to see that she and the child were what he wanted in life. He hoped he could communicate this commitment to her, and that it would come to be reciprocated, but he knew the process would have to be a gradual one.

Europe had kicked his ass.

His daughter was overjoyed to see him. Her love confirmed him in his resolve. He did not press his wife to make love that first night. In the morning, however, he found her returning from the bathroom to slip naked between the sheets with him.

The jet lag did not allow h m to do more than doze a little after that. He finally gave up on sleeping it off all at once and went to the office to open the accumulated mail. There were mounds of it of course. He would not even begin to answer it today. It was enough just to organize what had to be done.

He was frankly pleased with himself. There had been other European trips near the end of which he had drunk himself into such a condition that he could not venture from the house for four days upon returning. He seemed to have learned a lesson. This time he had not allowed a drinking spree to turn into a disabling binge even during the most manic or depressive of times. He had made it back sufficiently sane and healthy to begin at once the process of putting his house in order.

The insane jealousy struck unannounced that very evening.

He had parked in back, as usual, and he came around into the front yard of the apartment building to find his daughter riding on the shoulders of a handsome young man he could not remember ever having met. "Hi, Christa," Jimmy said, but his daughter paid him no attention-- she was having too good a time on the other man's back. Brenda came from the apartment, a bit too hastily it seemed to him, saying, "This is Christa's father. Jimmy, this is Don. He's staying in Apartment Two."

Against Christa's wishes, the young man set her down and took Jimmy's hand in a firm grip: "Hear you've been abroad. Good time?"

"Some of it."

"You have a beautiful daughter. And wife."

"I think so,' Jimmy said, turning towards the door,

"Be seeing you, I'm not working regularly so I'm around a lot."

I'll bet you are, Jimmy thought.

He knew then he would have to keep his eyes open. Bad timing. Complicate things. For the first time in years he would have to pay attention to what was going on around him, try to notice any little irregularities, clues, tip-offs.

What a pain in the ass.

One night soon they argue over dinner. Brenda makes the mistake of remarking, "All the new neighbors are nice to Christa," and Jimmy barks back, "All the new neighbors are loud."

"These apartments have always been loud."

"They're louder now and their occupants are partial to motorcycles and lowered suspensions and cocaine and beer busts outside our front windows."

"It's the summer weather."

"It's only April. It'll be summer weather through the World Series. We've outgrown this apartment."

"When I found that place in Belmont Shore last year, you said we were fine here."

"Christa was still in the crib."

"Christa loves it here."

"You love it here."

"I like being able to walk to Main Street or the beach. What other pleasures do I have?"

He looked away to where Christa was playing with a great mess of old blocks.

"Where'd she get those?"

"Don brought them over. He got them at a garage sale for a quarter."

Jimmy went to the refrigerator for the first beer of the day.

Two nights later he was sitting at twilight in front of the television with Christa in bed and Brenda finishing the dishes, when Don came out of Apartment Two wearing nothing but cut-offs and tennies, hopped a bicycle, and wheeled out of the yard. Brenda saw him too. In a couple of minutes she had dried her hands and caught Jimmy off guard with, "I feel like a walk to Main Street. Do you mind keeping an eye on Christa?"

"Of course not," he said, although of course he did. She went quickly out the door. Jimmy's adrenalin was flowing. Where the hell was she going? To rendezvous with Don? Make plans for seeing each other now that her old man had, inconveniently, returned. Feel each other up in the shadows like a couple of panting, sex-crazed teenagers?

He got up and paced the floor. Started out the

door, only to remember that he was stuck there with the child. How clever of her. Her mind must have been working overtime while his was occupied with the sports news.

He went to each window. No. They wouldn't have been foolish enough to have been anywhere within his view. No need to be.

He was standing in the doorway, awkwardly, when Don returned on his bicycle, alone, and waved hello, looking at Jimmy in that curious way he always seemed to.

Shortly thereafter she returned, said, "Thanks—I really needed that. I'm going to shower now."

She was in the shower a long time. Returned to the front room only long enough to announce that she was going to bed.

Later he took a walk to Main Street himself, to Casey's bar. Part of him wanted to drink the troubles out of his head. Another part thought there might be a clue there to what she had been up to.

He succeeded in getting stumbling drunk and in convincing himself that she might, instead of with Don or in addition to him, have been sleeping with his friend, the bartender, or with other friends and acquaintances of his.

The amateur detective stuff started the next day. He should have reminded himself of the two times before in his life when he had allowed himself to succumb to this craziness and how it had done him no good on either occasion. But the fever was rising. He was suffused with a pleasure like brandy. He was taking control of the situation.

He began searching her drawers, going through cancelled checks and credit card receipts and letters and bills, trying to find evidence of a trip, a loan, anything incriminating. All he could find was that she'd borrowed a thousand dollars from her credit union.

Could she have needed that much more than her regular salary and what he'd left her?

He did his best to return everything just as he'd found it, and he made a point of being seated at the counter reading when she returned home from work. But she hadn't been in the bedroom two minutes before she began opening and slamming doors angrily. When the noise stopped, he could feel her glare on the back of his head, but he did not look up from his book.

She stormed out of the house and took Christa grocery shopping with her.

That evening she took her purse to bed with her, left it on the footstool next to her pillow.

Jimmy sat up in the other room, drunk and getting drunker, unable to think of anything but that the evidence must be in the purse. Probably in her wallet. Eventually he got himself drunk enough to believe that he could take the wallet from the purse without her noticing it.

"What the hell do you think you're doing?"

"I was just getting a sleeping pill out of my drawer."

"The hell you were. You were trying to get into my purse. And you went through all my checks today, didn't you?'

"All right. So what if I did? You're the one who should be answering the questions.'

"What questions?'

"What have you been up to?"

"I don't know what you're talking about."

"You've been fucking around."

"Don't be ridiculous."

"Who is it?"

"You tell me."

"Then there is someone,"

"I don't see how I can convince you that there isn't. So believe what you like."

He was so enraged that he made the greatest tactical error of their relationship:

"Maybe we had better split up."

Quietly, determinedly, she spelled it out: "Maybe we had."

For a decade this had been his trump card, or, at least, his bluff: that he was willing to leave and she did not want him to. Now he'd played it and she had picked up the point.

He recouped the best he could: "You leave

then. Haven't you heard about women's lib? The man doesn't have to be the one to leave any more. This place would be just right for me."

"Okay, I'll leave."

"And leave Christa."

"Not a chance,"

"Then I'll leave and I'll take Christa."

"You don't have anyplace to take her."

"Rafe and his wife said I could stay there until I found a place and that I could bring Christa."

"When did you talk to them?'

"This afternoon."

"You're not taking my daughter."

"Then maybe we'd better talk."

They were both exhausted by now. Although she kept insisting that she didn't see why he was so obsessed by it, he finally got her to say once and for all that no, she wasn't fooling around with Don, she wasn't fooling around with anyone. She said the loan from the credit union was because he wasn't paying his share since the baby came. He said he would pay a strict half of everything from now on, but that she would have to remember that it was his home too. She said she would make a real effort to respect his place in the home. Her alarm went off, and an agonized look came over her face. She would have no more sleep before a day's work. As her wrath rose, Jimmy escaped to bed. It would be another unproductive day for him, but at least he would be able to sleep now.

This might have been the end of it, but it was not. For one thing, they had always been at war, and he was waging his with greatly reduced weapons now. If there was any balance of power left, it was an uneasy one.

Still, they did have two superb days in the Antelope Valley. The ride was much easier and shorter than Jimmy had realized--the little girl hardly had a chance to get restless. By early afternoon they had checked in at the motel, had obtained a map of the wildflower locations, and were parked alongside county roads for pictures of the poppies.

"Get one of Christa sitting among the flowers," Jimmy said.

"I thought you hated cameras."

It was true—he always had. And he'd been vocal on the subject.

"There's a time and place for everything," he said.

He remained calm throughout the desert afternoon of picture-taking. Back at the motel he cooled off in the pool before they went forth in search of a decent Mexican restaurant. They found one. Afterwards he sipped a beer in front of the t.v. while Brenda got their child ready for her crib. When Christa was finally asleep, they got naked for love and he found himself more excited by his wife's body than he had been since their earliest days together. His mind went out of him and, her tight buttocks beneath him, he was hard as a teenager for her. When they were done, he lay there hoping the act had said things to her she would not believe were he to speak them.

If so, they were both to forget them soon. There were just too many ambiguous circumstances for his already overstimulated consciousness. He would awake to find her leaving with the kids for a morning at the canyons. Or for breakfast on Main Street at the diner where he learned she had become something of a breakfast regular, often joined at her table by at least one somewhat simplistic young man that Jimmy had never taken very seriously, but now had to in spite of himself. She took the kids to the park to feed the ducks, or to the playground to play on the swings, or to the beach, or to one or another of the shopping malls or to her parents' place in the retirement community, or to lunch or happy hour with one of the women she worked with. He had never known her to be such a goer. And his attendance was not encouraged,except by his daughter, When he did tag along, it was so obviously out of possessiveness that he felt himself a public fool. Whether his horns were real or imaginary they had to be visible to the world.

The constant partying at the apartments continued. One night a young coke dealer (who was always, according to Brenda, genuinely friendly to Christa) partook of too much of his own product and, locked out by his soon-to-be wife, battered a hole in the door with a baseball bat.

Jimmy sat inside his own apartment fingering an ice-pick.

And Don would later concede that his friend the dealer suffered from something of a Napoleon complex.

At other times Jimmy might hear "Death to all nigger-lovers" from frantic voices on the staircase, only to reflect that his apartment alone did not house bigots.

The worst was when he heard some friends of the manager inquiring into the sexual availability of a woman whose description seemed to match Brenda's. The manager replied, "She's married and has a kid, but she doesn't seem to be happily married. Isn't that the tightest butt you'd ever hope to see. I wouldn't mind changing her light bulb." Jimmy stopped himself on the way to the door with a reminder that he did not know they were talking about Brenda, and even if they were, what had they said that was so terrible? And indeed when he awoke Brenda to confront her, she insisted that there had been another woman hanging around that fit the description even better.

Truman Capote said the only common denominator he ever discovered among mass murderers was tattooing.

Jimmy reflected that he was probably the only untattooed male in the apartment house. A few of the women sported them also,

---

His suspicions had also extended to his daughter's pediatrician, mainly because his wife always spoke so highly of him and because she had had to bring the child in to see him a number of times while Jimmy was in Europe. The day of Christa's next appointment, Jimmy got up late, sick from last night's drinking, and started drinking again right away. Fifteen minutes before the time of the appointment he got in his car and started across town to the clinic. Maybe there wasn't even any appointment. Maybe that was just a cover for some other rendezvous. Or, since it was an appointment so late in the day, he might catch the doctor leaving with her. He didn't know what he expected to find. He just knew he had to find out something soon or go crazy.

He had planned to just drive by the parking lot, scanning it for her car. He had planned an alibi in case she should see him, that he had been shopping for a better used car on the automobile row that was only a block away. But when he reached the clinic, she was just putting the kids into their car seats and she saw him. He cruised into the lot and forgot he had ever forged an alibi. "I was just in the area," he said, "and thought I'd take a look for you.

"You were spying on me."

A doctor he didn't recognize came out and looked curiously at his wife and at him. He wondered if that was the pediatrician.

His wife slammed the door and drove furiously from the lot. His drunkenness masked some of the humiliation but not all of it. He stopped at the first bar and started drinking rum-and-cokes. Got into a discussion of women with the oil worker on the bar stool next to him. There was something comforting about the country-western texture of their colloquy. They began buying each other drinks. Jimmy didn't even think about leaving until he realized he was just about plumb out of funds.

He came storming into the house, warning her not to push him an inch further. He loaded half of his clothes in the car, then decided to order her to move out instead. Called Rafe to see if he could move in there temporarily if he needed to.

Humiliated, he tried to throw the chest of baby toys through the plate-glass window, but tripped and fell on the rocking horse, He would have an enormous bruise and cut beneath his arm from where the springs gouged him, and a scar that might last for life, his only war wound.

Finally he took a couple of pills with the last can of beer in the house and awoke shortly thereafter to beg her not to leave him, to plead that his life would be an emptiness without her and the baby, that her body was the only one he'd ever wanted,

She refused to promise not to look for an apartment after work. As she went out the door, he popped a Valium but brought it back up, the only substance to the otherwise dry heaves. When his blood sugar plummeted, the suicidal stage set in, but he had never owned a gun, never even fired a gun, and he couldn't keep down any pills, and he couldn't even think about slitting his wrists, and he was at least sane enough not to want to chance any methods that might leave him an Ethan Frome. So he spent the next few hours on and off the phone to Rafe, and pacing the floor, and sipping ginger ale and nibbling saltines; and lying back down and getting back up, and dying for a drink but afraid another day of booze and he might lose his mind for sure, or that if she came home to find him drink in hand, it might prove the cocktail straw that broke the back of the two-humped beast.

He called the babysitter's house for the first time in his life and asked her to have his wife call when she picked up the baby, but she forgot to relay the message, so eventually he got in the car, hands cramped to the wheel, and found Brenda going into the supermarket. Probably she never meant to look for an apartment anyway. Where would she find one by the beach that she could afford? But he wasn't thinking that clearly, he just begged her to please come straight home when she finished shopping.

And she did.

He promised he would quit the hard stuff, and if that didn't do the trick he'd quit drinking altogether. He'd go to a psychiatrist if necessary. He knew he'd been paranoid, knew it wouldn't have been like her at all to have been fucking around. He hadn't been himself. She'd see that he would make things better.

She didn't give him the benefit of a smile or a kind word, but at least she didn't leave. Later in the evening he allowed himself a little cheap champagne. He got some sleep that night, and better sleep the next night.

He had a letter about this time from a very good poet, a bit older than himself, who said that it was only booze that had kept the women in his life from driving him crazy ever the years. But Jimmy has to write back that the booze used to help him also, but that lately he'd been losing back during the hangovers the advantages he'd gained the night before and then some.

And sure enough, a couple of days later, he got it into his head that maybe it was her principal she was sleeping with, and he started driving by her school and the nearby bars and motels.

Fortunately, she'd left work early and wasn't there to catch him.

One afternoon her best friend among her co-workers stopped by the house, and when Brenda was in the other room the friend beamed, "Don't you think it's wonderful how independent Brenda has become since she had the baby?"

It angered him that she was able to sleep now when he was not. He could remember the years when just the opposite had been true. And so he sat up writing letters to her now, articulate though gradually illegible essays upon passion, love, jealousy, respect, his hope of a future for them. One night he composed "A Clarification of Grievances":

"I have the feeling that the only interest you have left in me is monetary, that you are taking joy in bleeding me for my sins of the past.

"When you deliberately got pregnant, I advised you that I could not afford to have a child, and you said you could handle the brunt of the expense.

"You have maneuvered me into precisely the situation I have most feared all my life--a loveless, nearly sexless, petty, bickering marriage like that of my father and my mother, like that of your father and your mother.

"I told you I never wanted to be in a position

again where I had to have money constantly on my mind. You said I wouldn't have to. I said I never wanted to be in a position again where I would have to choose between my children in the distribution of support. You said I wouldn't have to.

"I am reduced again to financial worry, to lack of time and space for work, lack of love, too much drinking, and a marriage that is nearly indissoluble for financial reasons.

"You do not treat the children of my other marriages the way I want you to, the way they deserve to be treated.

"The more I give in to your financial demands, the worse position I am in to fight you or to leave you.

"If I fight you at night like this I can't sleep.

"Yet I can't risk my job, my sanity, my productivity, my friends.

"I've got to get away from you."

He always felt great as he went to bed after leaving such a daring and definitive letter for her. And he always shuddered to a horrified awareness in the morning. This time he was fortunate enough to wake before her and to consign the Declaration of Independence to the bottom of the trash.

One day, however, he became aware that she was only saving the incriminating letters, the loony or threatening or embarrassing ones, never the simple declarations of love for her and their daughter. So he searched the house until he found where she was keeping his notes, and he destroyed the most compromising ones. And he began to write on all his notes: "Permission is not granted for the preservation of this document."

Then he took to his office everything that he could not risk her destroying on the day when she'd discover he had gotten into her collections.

He also noticed that she never signed her own notes "Love" anymore and never said she loved him, although he always wrote "Love" on his communications and told her he loved her frequently. He nearly begged her to tell him that she loved him, and she finally did consent to say, "I love you, Jimmy," but with such a strain and weariness that he knew he'd never force her into saying it again.

He walked around now with a hollow feeling in the pit of his stomach, but the times were not of course monolithically bad. They spent a good two days in the old gold-mining town of Julian, perched beneath Palomar and above San Diego and Anza Borrego. Brenda had her hour of perusing the wildflower exhibition, and they introduced Christa to the old-fashioned drugstore soda fountain, They made love. They lavished love on Christa. Jimmy was as affectionate towards his wife as she would allow. She behaved towards him with a civility bordering on affection.

The euphoria did not last, though. Even Jimmy was shocked by the extent of her disdain for him on Father's Day.

He was not a great holiday person, and he was not a reliable gift-giver-- he was in fact hundreds of gifts behind towards family and friends. But with a daughter now he had made a point of buying Brenda Christmas and birthday and Mother's Day presents, And they were going to her parents' for Father's Day. He knew this was primarily to honor her father, but he'd sort of expected that a little of the spirit of the occasion might slop over onto him.

Instead she did not even encourage him to attend. And when he indicated he did plan on being there, she suggested he drive his own car so that she could take V. first to the canyons by herself. Since his car was so badly in need of a new carburetor that he could not depend on it even making the sixty mile round trip, he was not in favor of that idea.

So he tagged along on the ride to the wildlife sanctuary, while his wife made it clear that his presence was a blight on what could have been a good time. And when her parents asked him what he'd been doing for the summer, she interjected that he'd been sitting on his ass because of the grant he'd received, and that she couldn't wait to send him back to work. She hadn't bothered to get him a gift; with a little laugh she explained to everyone that she'd managed to forget that he was even a father.

That evening, with Christa asleep, he suggested sex, but she said she was too tired. He said that was okay, but to please lay off attacking him in front of his child and that since he was paying half the rent he would sit around on his ass just as goddamn much as he wanted.

She muttered a cold "Okay" and he let her go to bed.

But he was fired up now, so he walked to the Irish bar on Main Street." He got very drunk very quickly and started interrogating his bartender-friend, in what he hoped was not too transparent a manner, about Don and other neighbors of his who drank there. The bartender said that Don was a hustler of pool and older women, preferably with money, and that he didn't like him very much. Of course Jimmy was also suspicious of the bartender who he knew had always liked Brenda and found her extremly attractive and who he knew from other incidents had no compunction about sleeping with friends' wives. Later Jimmy would be unable to remember what he had said or been told beyond a certain point that night. He hoped he had not spilled his entire bellyful of fears.

At home, trying to remove his jeans, he tripped and landed on his ass on a little table by the bed, flattening it. Brenda jumped up and flipped on the light. He was sitting there in a drunken heap in what he figured was the low-point of his life: "Enjoy it," he said, "enjoy the spectacle. But you can't enjoy it as much as you'd like because I didn't break any bones. And now watch closely because I'm going to rise from my fall.

"Listen" he said, "you were weak and I taught you strength. Now you're going to have to watch me re-learn that strength from you."

With that he let himself collapse onto the bed and into sleep.

She was gone to work when he awoke the next day. He did not feel quite as bad as he deserved to, probably because he had eaten so well at the in-laws and thus was not, at least, drinking on an empty stomach.

He walked to the Dolphin Market for a newspaper, took the sports section into the bathroom with him.

He had taken as much pleasure as possible in the Lakers' World Championship victory over Philly. Now there wasn't much going on except baseball, and his team, the Yankees, for all the Steinbrener-Jackson-Martin shenanigans, got much less ink out here than the local teams. So he rooted for the Dodgers as long as they were winning, and had over the years learned to enjoy an Angels' loss almost as much as a Yankees' victory. Still the June sports pages were not a long read. On the back page of the section were the comics and the horoscopes. He had quit reading the funnies, even Doonesbury, years ago,, except sometimes the Sunday Andy Capp. He had never read the horoscope and had taken a special delight in ridiculing astrology around the mystically inclined. But since he hadn't decided how the day might best be spent, he took a desultory interest in the projection for Aquarians:"Bide your time in affairs of the heart. Meanwhile, get in shape," He could not remember a horoscope ever having had anything to do with his life up till now. He sat staring at the column for a while. Then he wiped himself, rose, and went to the closet to look for his running shoes.

Jimmy puts down The Longest Jet Lag, gets in his car and drives to a pay phone. He dials Laura at the University of the Northern Lights Graduate Dorms:

"Hello?"

"Laura?

"No, I'm one of her roommates. Laura isn't in right now."

"Do you know what time she'll be back?"

"I'm sorry but I don't. Can I take a message?"

"Tell her Jimmy called. I may call again."

"Tonight? It's quite late."

"I know."

He needs someone to talk to and he needs someone to sleep with. He would not mind sleeping with skinny blonde Argyle Harris, but he would not want to talk with her. He would not mind talking with his old friend Rafe, but he would not want to sleep with him. He goes to the bar where Rafe hangs out and finds him sitting there with Argyle Harris. He has one drink with them and then absents himself from their felicity.

"Laura?"

"Yes?"

"It's very late."

"It's a little late."

"No, it's very late."

"All right; it's very late."

"Where were you?"

"Oh, one of the women in the department had a little get-together, Was there some special reason you called? My head is spinning."

"Spinning? In other words, you've been at a party getting shitfaced."

"I'm mostly just tired."

"And we know what Laura gets when Laura gets drunk. When Laura gets drunk Laura gets horny."

"Jimmy, I really can't talk very freely right now."

"Because someone is with you?"

"Because my suite-mates are home."

"Then I'll do the talking. Listen, Laura, I was dying when we first started going out. I was eating away inside with the gastrointestinal acid of unhappiness. I had put in the most miserable year of my life, one of sadness, humiliation, and, if not actual impotence, then at least powerlessness. I kept myself going with a little work, a little exercise, care for my kids, hoping against hope that things would take a turn for the better. I read three horoscopes in three different papers each day just looking for promising signals. I did crazy things--sat up all-night with punk rockers pitching pennies at light fixtures, put the make on both halves of a Lesbian marriage, wandered in and out of Hollywood apartments where dope was lying all over kitchen tables and no one knew whether the former resident of the apartment was alive or dead or in hiding or in jail. I gave a poetry reading at a punk club, and I was afraid they'd think my stuff was laughably middle-class, so I read the most disgusting things I had ever written and you know what happened: the punkers were disgusted. I courted airheads, acid-freaks, and heavy-metal quasi-androgynes. I was wasting my life, but at least I was keeping myself from wasting away. I was looking in all the wrong places, but the looking kept me from giving up. Somehow I managed not to do anything so crazy as to get me thrown in jail or cost me my means of support or forfeit my intimacy with my children. The point is, though, that I was desperate.

"Then we started going out, and I knew you were what I needed, and I gave you all my concentration. We fought all the time, and I didn't turn into your faithful life's companion over night, but my life became basically good again, instead of essentially wrong, and I tried to repay you in whatever ways I could, and I was once again able to take control of my life.

"And then you said you had to get away, geographically at least, because you couldn't deal with my being married, in spite of all I'd told you about that marriage.

"I would have stayed if you had asked me."

"Asked you just to stay?"

"Well. . .

"Or asked you to marry me? Or said I would

move out on my family?"

"There was no future in it for me."

"So you conceive of your future as away from me? You're doing your best to move away from me. And if you don't already have someone else, then you're just waiting until he comes along?"

"You have no right to browbeat me. I don't have to apologize to you. I don't have to answer you."

"Oh, so now we get the declaration of independence of the liberated woman. You're up there and I'm down here, and for all you know I'm doing whatever I want, so you in turn feel free to do whatever you want. Is that it?"

"Jimmy, we shouldn't discuss these things when we're both tired and drunk. We should have learned that by now."

"Because the liberated woman is a dime a dozen, if I wanted a liberated woman I would never have ended up with you in the first place. Your great beauty, apart from your intelligence and physical attractiveness and simple good-naturedness and sense of humor, is that you're not just one more clone from the pages of Ms. magazine. You don't flaunt your liberation, or didn't when you were down here at least. I can't stop you from doing anything you want to do, but I can decide you're not the woman that I was in love with."

"For two years you refused to say you loved me. Even when I begged you to."

"I didn't want to say it under duress. I didn't want it to be taken as implying all sorts of practical commitments,"

"Call me some other time, Jimmy."

"Take two aspirins and call you in the morning?"

"We're not settling anything. I need some sleep."

"I've lost you, Laura."

He does need sleep. He pulls his car to the side of the road and lets himself doze off. He is soon caught up in a dream of being summoned to serve as altar boy at the entire slate of Sunday masses. But he can't answer that call to duty because he is in Laura's room, she is on her back on the bed that they pull down from the wall and he has been making love to her from every angle, and now he gets up, pulls her by her ankles to the side of the bed, and standing on the floor enters her and drives deep. He tucks her ankles behind his head and lifts her by the hips. Then he withdraws from her, kneels by the bed and lubricates her anus with his tongue. She gasps, but does nothing to dissuade him. He penetrates her asshole now, moving very slowly and pinching her nipple and rubbing her clitoris, and now she begins to exclaim, "Oh God, Oh God," and her thighs tighten on him and he falls forward on her as they come. . .

That was how it was with her at its best, which was often, and he does not know how he is going to do without it, without her.

He taught her how to enjoy a bottle of wine on a hot summer night in the top row of the Hollywood Bowl. She taught him Mozart; he taught her Coltrane. They taught each other a lot of literature. They told each other tales "of a harsh reproof, or trivial event that changed some childish day to tragedy." They walked among school children and he, forty-two, she, twenty four, they were school children.

He calls The Beautiful Redhead:

"Jimmy? Long time no hear."

"Yeah, well, you know. . .you divorced yet?"

"Oh yes,"

"Still seeing the same guy?"

"Unh-hunh.'

"You guys living together now?"

"No, he's working in San Francisco. I'm becoming a jet-setter."

"He in town tonight?"

"No."

"Well, how's about we go out for a couple of Chi-Chi's?"

"I'm flattered you remember my drink. But I don't think so. How's Laura?"

"She's going to school in the Great Northwest."

"Oh. You must miss her."

"Frankly I think she and I are kaput."

"Bad timing. I'm really locked in. Now a year ago I was crazy about you and you wouldn't even let me be in the same room with Laura. . ."

"I was crazy about you too. That's why I didn't want to put myself through situations where I couldn't compete for you. Where I'd have to watch my friends putting the make on you."

"Unh-hunh."

"You should be able to tell that that much at least is the truth."

"Okay."

"Listen. You remember that one afternoon in the car?"

"Which afternoon?"

"You know which afternoon. The afternoon you were just about naked and I had a finger or tongue in every orifice."

"You needn't be quite so graphic."

"That was just the start."

"It was also the highpoint."

"For Christ's sake, we both had spouses as well as other lovers. The logistics were impossible."

"Jimmy, a part of me would love to get together with you for Chi-Chi's and Cha-Cha's and Ooo-la-la."

"But another part. . .

"Enjoys even more telling you to get fucked,"

He wonders if he should try calling Carla,

Carla was one of the first girls with big tits that he had ever gone out with. It had taken them a while to get together, in spite of her making it clear with her big warm brown eyes that she was interested. It seemed he was always with Brenda when he would run into Carla. And then the first time she showed up at a bar when he wasn't with Brenda, she was with a mousy Platonic boyfriend--Platonic from her viewpoint. But her escort's aspirations were dashed when he crossed Gordoni the Crazy who sent Plato's glasses flying across the room. After that it was easy for Jimmy to detach Carla.

The boyfriend left, and he and Carla stuck around with Gordoni and other friends, playing trivia and singing Cole Porter songs. Then Jimmy walked her across the road to where she lived at the Stonehenge Garden Apartments. He was drunk and had a can of Bud with him, but she insisted he see the work-out room and sauna. That was okay--he'd worked out for years and had visions of using the Stonehenge facilities as her guest, but while she was around back opening up the place, the security guard had come by and Jimmy nearly was arrested, especially since he hadn't gotten around to learning Carla's last name yet and so could not say whose guest he was.

After she rescued him from the law, he amused himself showing off for her on the weights for a while. They never had very heavy weights in those polyurethane places anyway. He was able to toss around the heaviest dumbbell with one hand while sipping beer from the other.

If he were to try that stunt today, he'd probably have a heart attack.

When they got to her door, he started kissing her until she backed away and said, "You know, I can't possibly go to bed with you tonight. Why I don't even really know you." Since he didn't really want to arrive home with Brenda already up anyway, he just made a luncheon date for the next week.

On that occasion they consumed a bunch of halfbottles of Rhinecastle and played touchy-tweaky when the waitress wasn't looking. A couple of nights later they got drunk on Black Russians. Apparently she had gotten to know him a lot better in a week, because this time she went to bed with him.

The relationship had served its purpose quite well, for him at least, through its duration of a few weeks. They got to bed about twice a week, usually after playing a game in which he insisted he was already late home and she did everything possible to seduce him into staying longer, but with neither of them admitting that was her intention. Invariably they would end up outside her door, procrastinating and playing around and getting hotter all the time, until he would kiss her goodbye, grab her by the ass, and carry her to the bedroom. She would protest, "But you're going to be late," while he was tearing away at her clothes. Since they had in effect been fucking for the last two hours, it never took them long to get off. Then he'd lie next to her a respectable six or seven minutes before dressing and running. He didn't know whether she minded that, or whether she was just as glad to have had him and to still be free to enjoy the attentions of the single gentlemen around the pool.

Unfortunately he already had plans for a summer trip to Europe with Brenda. Well, Brenda was not planning to stay in Europe quite as long as he was. Carla seemed to have hopes of supplanting Brenda on the trip or, if not that, of joining him for the final month when Brenda would not be there. Jimmy even suggested it once, never expecting the response he'd get would be "Maybe I'll do that." Probably the beginning of the end for them was when he never repeated the invitation.

Even more than with Teri, everyone wanted to get into Carla's pants. Jimmy lost, or in some cases nearly lost, a lot of friends while he was going out with her. One guy had been a big-deal aerospace engineer, had brought back a beautiful French wife from Tahiti, had taken her and his kid on a yacht trip to the Bahamas, after which she'd dumped him for someone else. It wasn't hard to understand why. The first time you talked with him, he seemed an interesting enough fellow, but on each succeeding conversation it was here-we-go-over-the-same old-ground-again, Paris, Dostoevski, ersatz existentialism. He was shacked up with a new girl, much younger than his wife. The new girl wasn't very good-looking. She was skinny, nearsighted, had a prominent nose and bad skin. The guy was always talking about how beautiful she was, which was embarrassing for her and everyone else because they all knew that she wasn't beautiful. Then one evening, when Jimmy had got stuck across from the skinny girl at a table in the bar, he heard Gene whisper to Carla, "You'll be here Sunday at two then?"

So when they left he called her on it, and she said, "I was just trying not to hurt his feelings. I'm going to my parents Sunday. For Christ's sake, Jimmy, do you think I'd be interested in him."

Jimmy guessed that no, she wouldn't be, but he'd also have bet that she'd led the guy on with those Sicilian eyes of hers.

She wasn't at the bar that Sunday at three, but Jimmy was: "Listen, fucker," he said, "don't you ever try to pull anything with Carla again."

Gene said, "I'm sorry. I don't know what got into me."

"Okay. No apologies required. If it's not going to happen again, then it never happened the first time, as far as I'm concerned."

"Listen, man, I'm harmless. You know what happened last week? I took my wife to dinner at Francois' and afterwards I got her to a motel . . . and I couldn't get it up.

"So what? That happens to everyone."

"Don't try to make me feel better. I can get it up with Cindy, but I'm getting tired of Cindy."

"She's a beautiful girl," Jimmy said, a bit cruelly, but the engineer missed the irony.

"I know, man, I know, but you can imagine what sort of shape my ego's in. All I wanted was to prove to myself that I can still operate with a woman. I didn't have anything specific in mind . . . I just wanted to show myself that I could still make a date."

"Next time practice on some other guy's

woman, okay?"

"I'm sorry, Jimmy."

"For Christ's sake, stop apologizing. I feel worse about it than you do."

Another time one of his editors cornered Carla in his kitchen to announce, "If I weren't a happily married man, I'd be awfully hot for you."

The third incident was potentially lethal, as it involved the scion of a successful Sicilian-American clan. He was discussing Italian recipes with Carla, discussing them across Jimmy actually, and when he wrote down his address and phone number on a matchbook and passed it to Carla--so that she could invite him over to sample her cooking--Jimmy took it gently from her hand, ripped it into sixteenths, and handed the remnants back to him. Then they left before the young man had a chance to decide his family honor had been impugned. And Jimmy mailed him a postcard from Naples.

Near the end Carla made one last desperate attempt to fuck him up with Brenda. Brenda was out of town and he'd stayed the night at Carla's. When he screwed her that morning, she just ripped the shit out of his back. A little of that sort of thing goes a long way. But the real damage was oblique. He was so concerned with what his back looked like that he neglected to wash well before leaving Carla's place. Brenda arrived home that day and, in his passion for her, he impetuously unzipped and hauled out his cock. Brenda took one look and cried, "You're all blood!" He maintained it was always that color and stormed off, pretending his feelings were hurt. They didn't speak again for a week, It was incidents such as that one that helped their love along to the condition in which he now found it.

"Carla?"

"Yes?"

"Jimmy."

"Jimmy who?"

"Jimmy Abbey."

"Jimmy Abbey? . . . Ohhhhhh, Jimmy Abbey. Nice to hear from you. How was your trip to Europe?"

"Carla, that was ten years ago."

"Was it? I guess I should stop waiting for you to tell me when and where to join you then."

"Okay, okay . . . "

"It was nice while it lasted, Jimmy."

"It was."

"I've been married eight years."

"Happy?"

"You know."

"Is he there?"

"He will be in half an hour."

"I could be there in ten minutes."

Carla laughs: "No, Jimmy. It would be disappointing to us both to take a step backward, I think. But I've always wanted to ask you something."

"Yes?"

"I caught you with your eyes closed a couple of times when we were making love. Did you used to fantasize?"

"Only when you wanted it one more time and I wasn't really ready."

"What did you fantasize?"

"Different things, I suppose. Always about you, though. Honest."

"Tell me one scenario,"

"One is all I remember; You are hanging around the pool in your bikini, displaying your fleshly delights to the males of many ages flexing in the sun. A golden boy comes up to you, strikes up a conversation, and suggests you follow him into the weight room to see a new piece of equipment. There you find yourself surrounded by men and with the doors locked and the place soundproofed. These are the men of all ages who have been subjected to the frustrations of your magnetism, They bind you to an incline board and strip your flimsy garments from you. At first they are content to excite you with their hands and mouths

. . . but later they bring forth aerosol cans of a secret aphrodisiac stimulant. They apply the foam to your nipples, clitoris, vagina, and anus, and within seconds you are writhing in the grips of an intolerable excitation, begging them, pleading with them, screaming at them to satisfy you . . . Their answer is to apply more of the spray to you, while manipulating their own swollen organs . . ."

"Did you ever want to fuck my sister?"

"Yes."

"Did you ever put the make on her?"

"No. "

"Did you ever fantasize about being in bed with her?"

"I fantasized about being in bed with both of you."

"Goodbye, Jimmy."

He drives by a bar where he used to drink till closing and after closing regularly many years ago.

He doesn't recognize a face in the place.

The pool table is gone.

The foosball table is gone.

The pinball machine is gone.

An effeminate young man is playing Pac-Woman.

An ugly thirtyish woman is playing Pac-Man.

He says to the bartender, "You know, the zaniest betting pool I was ever a part of took place after hours in this joint years ago. We bet on what kind of animal Cal Worthington's dog would be."

"Wouldn't it be a dog?"

"No, it was never a dog. It was always some other kind of animal."

"Who was Cal Worthington?"

"He was a used car dealer. Did his own commercials. He 'would stand upon his head till his face was turning red to make a deal.' And he always had his dog with him, which was always some other kind of animal."

"What did you bet it would be?"

"A pig."

"What kind of animal won?"

"A goat. Others bet on gorilla, anteater, mouse."

"Mouse?"

"Cal had already used up a lot of the more likely animals."

"How much you lose?"

"A buck."

"Just a buck?"

"And a beautiful woman whom we all had just met and who left with the guy who guessed the goat. But I stopped at a coffee shop on the way home and ran into a woman I knew and she ended up giving me a blow-job in her car. She was working on a technique of holding balls and all in her mouth. That's the way things were a few years ago."

It's hard to tell whether the bartender is

incredulous or mildly disgusted. "We run a nice quiet bar here now. And no after-hours."

"Yeah, quiet," Jimmy says, getting up from the bar and picking up what he might have left as a tip, "and no before or during hours either."

He drives to the theatre on Main Street to see what's playing. The marquee reads, THE PRIEST'S NUN'S TAIL.

"A movie?" he asks the ticket girl. "Live," she says.

"Big crowds?"

"It's been playing for a week and you're the first customer."

He goes inside. There's a nun sitting on the stage on a simple chair. Another chair is empty. "Come on up and sit yourself down," says the nun.

Jimmy says, "I'd know that Upstate New York idiom anywhere. Aren't you. . ."

"Jane Goodcall. Your old girlfriend who became a nun and went off to Africa."

"Did you get gang-banged by savages?"

"Why is that the first thing I always get asked?"

"I don't know. Did you?"

"Yes."

"They got a lot farther than I did. You wouldn't even kiss me, until the last time I saw you. But you let Jim Burke kiss you after that dance."

"My God, are you still jealous of a kiss that occurred nearly twenty-five years ago?"

"Why did you kiss him when you wouldn't kiss me?"

"He didn't give me any choice and you did."

"And I gave you a choice and the savages didn't.'

"Watch it or I'll call my pimp."

"Who's your pimp?"

"Father Black."

"But I thought. . ."

"In show biz you roll with the tide. This is his latest barnstormer. Okay, what can I do for you?"

"I can't pay you."

"Then I can't do anything for you. Too bad--you look like you could use a little something."

"You're ancient."

"A year older than you. And centuries wiser. You want a little free advise?'

"Can I get anything else free?"

"No."

"Then I'll take the free advice."

"Political Involvement."

"What?"

"Get politically involved. It will keep your mind off sex and provide you with a sense of spiritual fulfillment, even as it opens sexual possibilities."

"I don't have the aptitude for activism."

"You don't care about your fellow man?"

"Actually I do care. And I stay informed. And I'll write political when something political occurs to me that everyone else isn't already saying."

"Go to Africa."

"I'd like to go to Africa to see the animals, but not to save the souls. A friend of mine went to Africa in the peace corps and she was back within a month with malaria."

"Then go to hell."

"See you there."

"Look, Jimmy, before you go, would it make up to you for my having let Jim Burke kiss me when I wouldn't let you, if I were to hike up my skirts and relive for you the experience of being gang-banged by the African savages?"

"Nothing could make up for that. It confirmed me in a burgeoning cynicism which is sometimes mistaken by the imperceptive for misogeny."

On the way out of the theatre he notices that the girl behind the popcorn counter has a pretty face. She is overweight but she dresses nicely, intelligently, wearing, for instance, boots and skirts and blouses that promote her ample bosom while drawing attention from her breadth of lower back. And she does seem to have lost a little weight. "When do you get off?" he asks her.

"Oh, I can probably start shutting the place down in about half an hour."

"Well, look, since I'm the first patron this week, and even I didn't buy any popcorn, why don't you start shutting down now, and I'll go next door and buy a bunch of canned Harvey Wallbangers, and then I'll come back and pick you up and we can go drink the drinks in my car and fool around just like a couple of teenagers."

"Sounds like a plan.'

Coming out of the liquor store, he runs into Cowboy Bill. Cowboy Bill has been on a three-month binge. He says he's going to quit the day after New Year's Day and stay on the wagon until St. Patrick's Day. He is in mourning for the loss to another man of his woman of ten years, a rising stock-broker who also garnered a number of first-places in wet t-shirt contests. Jimmy's always liked both Cowboy Bill and his girlfriend a lot. He hates to see the Cowboy in his present condition, eyes swollen like barrel cacti after a summer thunder-storm, but he knows this is a thing that Bill must work through in his own way.

"You can only push a good woman just so far," Bill says, "or sooner or later you'll wear out her tolerance,"

Jimmy knows what he means, and that it's even truer for women who aren't that good.

"I backhanded a woman for the first time in my life tonight," Cowboy Bill says,

"Marge?"

"Yeah. She slid right on down the hood of her car. I thought to myself, 'She must have had her car waxed or she wouldn't be sliding like that.' Ain't that a helluva thing to be thinking when you've just smacked the woman you love."

"She okay?"

"Oh sure. I picked her up and she cried and I cried and then I kissed her goodbye again."

"Hard times all around."

"Last week a friend of mine asked me to do a little collecting, not much, a hundred bucks or so, and I didn't have anything better to do so I stuck a .22 in the back of my belt and went and made the collection, no problem at all, but after I delivered the money I forgot I still had the gun tucked back there and later that night I was drinking beer outside with some people and this balloon came floating down the street, dancing along some wind currents, and I drew that gun like Tom Mix and shot that damn balloon dead on the spot. Sure did gain me a little respect."

"Like the time you chainsawed down the middle beam of the Gold Rush Saloon."

"Yeah, and the police were real polite to me, but they beat the shit out of that poor black guy from the V.A. hospital that just happened to be handling my shotgun when they walked in."

"Well, be careful driving, Bill,"

"Sheee-it, you think any cop's gonna give a 502 to someone who looks as gung-ho American as I do?"

The Cowboy is probably right.

He and Trinka have a canned Harvey Wallbanger in the front seat of Jimmy's Toyota and then he starts kissing her and running his tongue inside her ear and playing with her tits. She opens her blouse for him to suck on them and bite the nipples. But when he tries to reach beneath her skirt, she stops his hand.

So they have another canned Harvey Wallbanger, and she tells him about the thyroid problem that went undetected for so long and how much better she feels, how much more energy she has, now that she's on thyroid pills.

Then they start over again, but this time she lets him do everything but pull down her pantyhose.

They have another canned cocktail and she tells him how her mother, sick with heart disease herself, flipped out and had Trinka's horse of eight years, in perfectly good health, destroyed. This at a time when Trinka already thought she was going nuts from the undetected thyroid deficiency.

This time she pulls the pantyhose down for him and urges his hand up into her and guides him and cheers him on until she comes. Then she goes down on him, expertly.

While they have the last of the cocktails, she

says, "It's too bad that my car is even smaller than yours. And that I live so far away."

"No, it isn't," he says. "I liked it just fine the way it was."

"Will I see you again?'

"Probably," he says. "You see, what I'm looking for is an Interim Girlfriend. Because I'm not sure whether I still have a Real Girlfriend or whether I have to look for a new one. But if I have to look for a New Real Girlfriend, I want to warn you that it will probably not be you. However, whether I have the Same Real Girlfriend or a New One, you can always be an Interim Girlfriend as long as you don't mind only seeing me when I want to see you, and only going the places with me that I want to go with you, and not letting anyone find out about us, and limiting our sex to what can be accomplished in the front seat of your car or mine, because this sort of sex fills a definite psychic need that I developed in my high school years."

Trinka says, "All right."

"And if you see anyone else I don't ever want you to allude to it or to let it interfere with your seeing me, and if you catch anything you'd better warn me."

"All right."

"Fine, then, I think we can have a very romantic and mutually satisfying thing together, on an Interim basis; let me see you to your car."

He calls Laura, "Are we necessarily kaput?"

"No," she says. "I never said we were. I may be back, you know. Incidentally, when I was moving out of my apartment, there was a football sitting on my front lawn. Was it yours?"

He drives to her former apartment. Sure enough the football is still sitting on her front lawn. He gathers it lovingly into his arms.

He parks across from the stadium. Jogs through the gates and onto the playing field. Sets the ball on the opposing team's twenty yard line.

The opposing team breaks its huddle. Jimmy is lined up across from the tight end, Whizzer Quisenberry. His back aches; his gut nearly touches the ground; his arms have grown thin as chopsticks. But though he has the ailments of middle-age, he retains the instincts of a whippersnapper. He anticipates the hike-count, sidesteps Quisenberry, and is in the enemy backfield a fraction of a second after the football. He smashes into the quarterback who is just setting up in the pocket. The ball pops loose and into the air. Jimmy cradles it with both arms, like an old-time fullback, and lugs it, one painful step at a time, into the end zone. He tosses the football definitively over his shoulder and continues his jog towards the western gate. As he leaves the stadium. he raises two fistfuls of fingers in a gesture intended to mean, "I'm Number Ten." He knows he is not even Number Ten, but that is all the fingers that he has.

At the souvenir stand he purchases the only items that have nothing to do with football, a Mickey Mouse Doll and a White Monkey Doll. He gets in his car and drives home. His wife is just about to put herself and the kids to bed.

"Mickey Mouse, Mickey Mouse, Mickey, Mickey, Mickey," his three-year-old son squeals.

His wife is in a better mood than usuals: "It must be ESP. He's been begging me for a Mickey Mouse doll all day."

"And did you bring my Minnie Mouse?" his daughter asks,

"No, he says, "it seemed to me that Minnie had a sort of second-rate role in those stories, definitely a supporting part, and I don't ever want you to have to play secondfiddle to anyone. So I bought you the most beautiful doll that I could find, the White Monkey Doll."

"I love it," she says, "I love you."

"I love you, Jimmy," his little boy says. "And I love Mickey too."

His wife takes herself and the kids off to the bedroom then. He can hear her reading them a bedtime story.

He pours himself a glass of Manischevitz Extra Heavy Malaga wine. He knows he has to stop drinking such sweet stuff or he'll end up with diabetes like his father, and that is not the way he wants to go. He's got to find some kind of exercise too, one that won't throw out his back.

And he has His Work to do.

He pours himself a second glass of wine and takes it with him to the typewriter. He takes from his shirt pocket a compressed stack of loose notes. He says to himself, "I bet I can cook up a little something out of these." He puts a blank sheet in the typewriter and types in the center of it:

THE POCKET BOOK
A Novel by Jimmy Abbey

The Art Angel

After the first class he came to the desk and asked, "Professor Abbey, I'm a graduate student in the Art Department. Do you think I'll be able to keep up with this class?"

"Have you had any poetry writing classes before?"

"A long time ago."

"Have you been writing since then?"

"Oh yes.

"Then I can't guarantee anything, but I doubt there will be any problem. In the past I've found that students from art often do more interesting work than the English majors because they're more used to experimentation. What sort of art do you do?"

"It's hard to describe but, yes, it's certainly experimental."

"I hope I can see it sometime."

"I'd be honored."

"Have you checked with an advisor to make sure this course will count towards your degree?"

"Oh yes, but I would have taken it anyway."

"And your name?"

"Owen Thomas."
"Can't get more Welsh than that."
"But I was adopted."
"Still, have you read Wilfred Owen and Edward Thomas and Dylan Thomas and Gerard Manly Hopkins?"
"Oh yes."
"Then you should do just fine in here. And if I'm very wrong it will no doubt become painfully apparent to both of us rather quickly."

"Thank you, sir."

"No problem, Owen."

How old was Mr. Thomas?
Jimmy was terrible at such estimations, but he guessed thirty five, maybe older, probably, judging by wrinkles, mottling, bentness, politeness . . . forty.
How was he dressed?
Worse than Jimmy, who was notoriously, professionally unkempt. Paint-stained windbreaker and loose white pants. Sockless. Ancient tennies. A cap of the sort associated with the other type of painter.
What were Jimmy's first impressions of Mr. Thomas?
In the course of nearly thirty years of teaching, Jimmy had learned to dispense with first impressions. Too often the punkest students had turned out the most gentle, sensitive, talented, intelligent. Seeming troublemakers had ended up the most

loyal of his drinking buddies. Disaffected ones who had never had an A in their lives had achieved perfect exam scores. The most shy of the ladies had shown the stoutest of hearts. There may have been some modicum of truth to some stereotypes in the general population, but in teaching you had to grant each new face a clean slate.

After the third class meeting, Mr. Thomas followed Jimmy to the Servomation machines. He cuddled a paper cup of black coffee in what Jimmy noticed were hands stained and grimy with art.

"I've bought the books for your first assignment," he said.

"I hope they're of use to you."

"I'm learning a lot from them. I'll buy the others as soon as I can."

"That's fine."

"There's an exhibit of kinetic installations opening in Gallery C tomorrow."

"I'll try to get to it, but it seems the second I hit campus, every hour is overbooked. I'm late to my office hours now and there will be a line of students waiting for program advisement. I love to wander around the art buildings, but it's a pity how seldom I find the free time to do it."

"Well, I'm already learning a lot from your class. Could I hand in my first two poems early?"

"I'd really appreciate it if you could. The sooner the class can focus on specific poems the better. Do you have an installation at the exhibition?"

"Oh no, I'm not quite ready for that yet."

Owen Thomas's first two poems left the other students speechless. Since Jimmy never allowed himself to be caught at a loss for words, he went on at some length about the seafaring imagery, the correct yet varied iambics, the repetitions of long vowel sounds -the exclamation "ah" in particular-functioning partly to spring the rhythm in a manner reminiscent of Hopkins and partly as a tempo indicator and surrogate punctuation mark in the way Joyce had employed "yes" to bring Molly Bloom's soliloquy and, indeed, Ulysses to a climax. "Thank you, Owen," he concluded. "These are excellent models so early in the class of traditional techniques and versification employed with flexibility as part of a distinctly individual style." The other students stared at Jimmy as if either he was putting them on or they had better start filling out drop-slips. Owen Thomas, who had already established permanent residence in the back row by the windows, lowered his gaze but could not prevent the hint of a smile from invading his features.

There were other talented poets in the class as well, Jimmy was soon to discover, not at all to his surprise, but they all wrote much more like each other, even granted considerable differences of style and subject matter, than they did like Owen. Owen contributed with his syncopating "ah's" and "yay's" and "amen's," his visionary wanderings upon a single secret cosmic sea, his tolling echoes from all the monumental religious poets from Ecclesiastes and the Anglo-Saxon elegists through Donne and Blake to Hopkins, Yeats, Eliot, and his namesake. He seemed to have embarked on a sequence of interlocking and accretive odes, and Jimmy pointed out to the mute classmates that it had always been endemic with visual artists to explore thematic fields to their exhaustion whether it be Venuses or Madonnas or Waterlilies or Coke Bottles or the Ocean Park semiabstractions. In the back row by the windows, Owen nodded in agreement.

Often he lagged behind after class to follow Jimmy towards the food machines, but he never imposed himself unless spoken to first. Then he might mention exhibitions here and there throughout Southern California that the teacher knew he would never get to, but that he made a point of publicizing to the class. Occasionally he would make a revealing or enigmatic comment concerning a poem by one of his fellow students such as, "I know what he means because I grew up in Beverly Hills," or "I was raised an Episcopalian also," or "You're right about the general futility of political poetry," or "You're right to warn the young people that drugs won't help their art." He never alluded to drinking, as if he knew that alcohol was Jimmy's personal drug of preference and privilege and as if it might once have played a (probably minor) role in his own life. In class he laughed unpredictably but privately. When Jimmy asked him what art projects he was working on, he would describe them enthusiastically, but Jimmy did not really have the expertise or visual imagination to grasp them. And Jimmy was, of course, always too busy, albeit legitimately so, to get anywhere near the art complex.

In mid-semester an unfortunate although minutely subtle series of events occurred. Jimmy had established a system of distributing the workshop poems to the class in which the students left their stacks of Xerox copies on his desk and then, well into the class, when he was pretty sure anyone who was planning to attend was seated, Jimmy would begin what he immodestly referred to as "the patented distribution process," which he adamantly, though tongue-in-cheek, insisted would account for the bulk of their grades. Owen had fallen into the habit of wandering into class a minute or two after Jimmy had begun to teach and standing between Jimmy and the class as he selected his copies of the poems off the tops of the stacks. Although the jaws of the other students had fallen agape in dismay, Jimmy had tried patiently to explain that the poems would be distributed in a few minutes to the entire class. Owen didn't seem to hear him. Eventually the unwelcome ritual caught Jimmy on a day that had gone particularly badly and he snapped, "Owen . . .

please, just take your seat . . . I'll be passing out the poems to the entire class as soon as we finish discussing this poem."

"Oh," Owen said and turned towards his corner. A surfer girl to his left caught Jimmy's eye and rolled her own. Afterwards Jimmy would not be able to reconstruct the extent to which he had reciprocated her gesture--certainly he had not rolled his eyes, but had he raised an eyebrow, shrugged even-so-slightly his shoulders, let any shadow of a recognition of Owen's essential Otherness pass over his countenance? He hoped not and, anyway, Owen could not have been aware of any such betrayal unless he literally had eyes in the back of his head. Or antennae. Or some sort of sixth sense such as true paranoids--and true artists--are sometimes rumored to possess.

Whatever the case he was not in attendance the next week and when he returned he stared at his desk, no longer speaking, not even to himself. Jimmy thought he had fallen a couple of poems behind in the assignments as well, although, in truth, it had been twenty years since Jimmy had kept any formal record of such things.

These were, in fact, not the best of times in Jimmy's life. It only occurs to the most sensitive of students that their teachers have lives of their own, and that, in those private lives, they or their loved ones may be ailing or broke or breaking or dying. But admit weakness as a teacher and the majority of students will be howling for your blood. Jimmy had seen it happen to colleagues. Past popularity never mattered because the majority of the students would not have been around in those days. Like professional goalies or quarterbacks or relief pitchers, you were only as good as your last outing. There were times that mid-semester that Jimmy could barely climb the single flight of stairs to his classroom, let alone put other domestic problems out of his mind. But he knew it was a case of, What have you done for the taxpayers lately? All experienced teachers knew this. He dragged his ass up the stairs, let their mostly fledgling poems displace his loved ones, and never let them see him sweat.

Of course it was a rough time of the semester for the students too. He could tell from one young lady's evasive medical explanation of two weeks of absence that she had undergone an abortion. Boyfriends and girlfriends and husbands and wives were rampantly rejecting each other. The surfer girl and a flamboyantly effeminate young man exchanged a volley of insinuations regarding various orifices and bodily fluids, and Jimmy had to spring into intervention like a referee of a hockey match. Whenever Jimmy's attention was drawn to Owen Thomas's dour corner, he felt bad for the counterproductive turn their semester had taken, but he seldom had long to dwell on it.

And then one dreary late-November Thursday when two poems were due, Owen handed in six. And while continuing the trademarks of the earlier work, they had risen to astonishing heights of virtuosity, power, originality, spiritual vision. And unsatisfied as usual with Jimmy's comments, the most literal-minded young man in the class turned directly to the artist and demanded, "Can you or can you not paraphrase these poems for me?"

And Owen said, "Oh no, of course I can't do that."

And Jimmy resisted the impulse to launch into a recapitulation of the old dispute of Yvor Winters with Hart Crane's work and instead allowed the interrogation to proceed to, "But you did have something in mind that you were hoping to communicate to us?"

"Oh yes."

"Then what at least approximately was it?"

"Well," Owen Thomas began, "you would have to imagine that you were standing with one foot in Norway and the other in Guatemala and that your heart was in St. Petersburg and your hands in Grenada and San Juan Capistrano. You would have to know what each religion that ever existed has ever signified and in what relation to each other all religions stand. You could not, of course, have heard God's voice, but one would hope you would have heard at least the echoes of the echoes of each of the choirs of the angelic orders. To have read Rilke and Lorca would not be sufficient; you would want to have been in personal though whispered dialogue with them. Not to mention planetary plate tectonics. . . "

After who-knows-how-many minutes Jimmy interrupted with, "I think what Mr. Putnam was asking, Owen, is where you get these ideas from. Are there books, for instance, where we could read up on these things?"

"Oh no," Owen beamed, like a Magus to a novice, "there are no written documents."

"Would you say, perhaps, that we should just live and listen?"

"Yes," Owen nodded happily, 'just live and listen--that's it exactly."

That night Jimmy told his wife, "It was as if he was saying, 'I knew that I could count on you!'"
"Did the other students make fun of him?"

"No, I think they understand now that he is in another world from theirs, and not one to be despised."
"You don't think he's a madman?"
"I think he's a genius."

After the last class, he followed Jimmy to the food machines and, when Jimmy recognized him with, "You added immeasurably to the class, Owen; the students and I are profoundly in your debt," he said, "If I ever achieve your eminence, Professor, I hope I will comport myself like you."
Jimmy was thrown off guard. He scanned the other's face for irony but found none. "Will you be back on campus next semester then?" he blurted.

"I don't think so."

"No problem with grades, is there? You'll get an A from me."

"Thank you. I think my other grades will be B's. I've learned a lot from my art instructors and I think they like some of the work I've done, but they advise me that their graduate program is really designed for art educators and that it would be better if I moved on to a program more oriented to studio artists."

"Will they continue your grant if you don't?"

"I don't think so."

"Can you afford one of the art schools?"

"If they give me aid."

"Do you think they will?"

"I hope so."

The bastards, Jimmy thought. The lousy stinking, hypocritical, pedantic, cowardly bastards. Of course he'll never be an "art educator." Could Van Gogh have been one? Could Neruda have taught creative writing? Could Christ have chaired a Religious Studies department?

But what more, Jimmy thought, am I going to do for him? I won't even consider inviting him over for Christmas dinner because I'm too protective of my kids.

Jesus, Jimmy thought, I hope he's not some sort of Art Angel sent down like in a Jimmy Stewart or Wim Wenders movie or a Magritte painting to provide me with a test by which my eternal fate will be determined.

"Listen, promise me you'll keep writing the poems."
"Oh yes, I intend to."
"You have a very considerable sequence going."
"I know."
"Find a way to integrate the poems into your canvases. Poetry publications are notoriously ephemeral and that will give what you write an extra shot at permanent availability."
"You mean immortality."
"Okay, that's what I mean."
"I'm always working to integrate all aspects of my art."
"I'm sorry I never got to one of your exhibitions."
"There will be others."
"Look, I have to get up to the office."
"Thank you for everything you've done for me, Professor Abbey."
"De nada, Owen."

That night Jimmy's wife asked him, "Do you think you'll ever hear of him again?"
"You mean do I think he'll make it?"
"Yes."
"No, not unless he really is some kind of saint. Otherwise, for all his brilliance, he is just one more of the destroyed ones of the second half of the twentieth century. The odds his life have stacked against him are insuperable. The good who die young are the lucky ones."

Pescado Veracruz

My wife took it wrong once when she apologized that she and my son would not be able to go out to eat with me that evening, and I replied, "But I like to eat alone." I do enjoy dining with her, and I enjoy any time spent with my children, but I have also, always, taken pleasure in the solitude of eating alone in restaurants. Not in all restaurants—I don't, for instance, enjoy eating where I am not wanted or in stuffy surroundings—but in restaurants where I am comfortable. These are most often the places where I am recognized as a regular customer and one who compensates for the modesty of the single-diner's bill by overtipping. In such places I am able to eat exactly what I want, at my own pace, and, simply, to think. I always used to eat with a sports section in one hand, but I don't do that anymore. Nowadays, I only bring a book along if I anticipate a significant wait in being served. Otherwise I look and listen and think and, occasionally, jot an idea for a story or a poem.

Yes, I always took food seriously, but all-the-more-so now that I only eat one real meal a day and have forfeited the pleasure and the penances of alcohol. With this regimen I have personally evolved, coupled with the daily exercise of a swim or an extended walk with the dog, I have shed over a hundred pounds and have, more significantly, kept them off. I eat nothing until late afternoon or early evening, consuming in the meantime copious quantities of Diet Pepsi. I allow myself some dried fruit before bedtime, filling and an excellent source of fiber.

This afternoon, for instance, I am eating at a Mexican restaurant on Pacific Coast Highway that specializes in large portions at reasonable prices. I am having the Pescado Veracruz, a sort of fish fajitas served in a sizzling skillet of onions, green peppers, and tomatoes, with rice, beans and cheese, a dollop of guacamole, a bit of salad, and a radish. I have already consumed a bowl of large tortilla chips dipped in a succession of smaller bowls of salsa. I add extra hot sauce to the fish, the beans, the rice. This strikes me as an exemplarily nutritious and balanced meal—the place fries with canola oil, not lard—although I have of course taken my daily assortment of vitamins and minerals before leaving the house.

The restaurant, though catering to families both Anglo and Mexican, is on a rather rough stretch of the legendary highway. I gaze upon the parking lot of a cheap motel to which, I must admit, I escorted a succession of young women in my wilder years. Today it seems to serve largely as a haven for transients and prostitutes and drug dealers. The teen-aged dealers and their clientele are virtually interchangeable. All wear backpacks. They move behind walls out of sight for the actual exchange of goods for cash, but they are far from paranoidally superstitious. The prostitutes who patrol the highway are remarkably unattractive and seem twig-thin with AIDS. Nowadays, the best-looking streetwalkers are the police-women who entrap the johns whose names are subsequently published in the local paper. Haven't we become an upstanding community?! I never patronized whores in my native country anyway—only in Mexico and Europe where there are more reliable ground rules. I almost did on a couple of drunk, horny, and depressed occasions, but I chickened out, mainly from lack of familiarity with the local protocols. This was no doubt all for the best.

I am not currently tempted by the sexual or pharmaceutical offerings of the neighborhood.

The waiter, a young Chicano, refills my Diet Pepsi and provides new bowls of chips and salsa.

Police cars cruise by regularly. They show no concern with the illicit commerce of the area. Such enforcement is relegated to sweeps by task forces. They do pull an occasional motorist to the side of the road, possibly after running a check of stolen cars, fugitives, and outstanding warrants. The area was notorious at one time for uninstigated police brutality until a widely publicized incident in which a black football star at the college hanged himself (or was hanged) in his cell, precipitating a federal investigation. A new style of enforcement has coincided with the wooing of car dealerships and discount outlets in the cause of substantial tax base.

Times change. And we change with them.

The bill comes to $8.95. I will leave a tip of $1.95, which somehow strikes me as less ostentatious than two dollar bills. I will pilot my four-year-old Taurus, still running smoothly, down the hill and around the hazardous traffic circle. I am pleasantly surfeited but not overstuffed. At home I think I'll read an Anglo-Indian novel for an hour, then watch the Tony Awards with my wife and son. Near the end of the telecast I'll allow myself some figs or dates or raisins. Washed down, of course, with Diet Pepsi. I'll be in bed by midnight. Busy day tomorrow.

I wonder if a young lady today, or even a slightly less young one, would settle for a cheap motel room along the P.C.H. Might have to up the ante to a Motel-6. How different would it be without the alcohol? Not a good time to find out right now. Maybe in a year when the boy has gone away to college. Empty nest. Survey the prospects. No rush. Cross that bridge when we come to it. Wild times those were. Good memories to have. Dionysiac. Before the feminists ripped Orpheus's head off and sent it bobbing down the flood channel. Times change. And sometimes they change back.

Cell Phone

It is the Sunday after Thanksgiving, one of the busiest travel days of the year. Jimmy and his wife have come to Los Angeles International Airport to meet the plane which is carrying their high school son back from a weekend's stay with their college daughter. The flight is, predictably, delayed. They are standing in line at Starbuck's in hopes of purchasing a multigrain scone or a honey-bran muffin. They are not conversing at the moment, partly because each is a worrier as regards their children, partly because they get along better when they don't talk, and partly because each is looking forward to his (and her) caloric treat / indulgence / reward .

A man in front of them, however, is speaking into his cell phone. He is speaking in the loud voice of one of those involved in "the industry," Hollywood, one of those who may not actually live in California but who, if he does, probably lives on the "Westside," the side nearer the ocean. In L.A., the affluent have fled to the west, but, unless a platform should be built over the water or, as many have done, they move to Maui or

Kauai, they cannot flee any farther. People who live in the other communities of Southern California—the San Fernando and San Gabriel valleys, Long Beach, San Pedro, Watts, East L.A., Downey, Torrance, and so forth—are much less apt to speak loudly, ostentatiously, proudly into cell phones. They are more apt simply to hope that their cell phones are working when their cars break down on the freeway after dark.

The man seems to be talking to a daughter from whose mother he is divorced. "No," he says, "I'm at the airport . . . LAX . . . it's packed . . . yes, well, look, I only have a couple of minutes, I'm waiting in line for coffee . . . what am I doing in L.A.? . . . I've been visiting Franci . . . Franci, you know, the new woman I've been seeing, I told you about Franci . . . I didn't? . . . I'm sure I did, you just weren't listening, you just weren't paying attention, you were probably running off somewhere, that's why I don't call more often because, you see, when I do you always seem to be in a rush to be doing something else . . ."

I'm going to take that phone, Jimmy thinks, of which you are so proud and I'm going to bash your brains in with it.

". . . yes, yes you do . . . well, anyway, I don't intend to argue it with you but what I wanted to tell you is that Franci, my new girlfriend, I'm sure I told you about her, she's wonderful, beautiful, I'm very serious about her, well the point is she has a daughter who's just your age, yes, eleven, terribly bright, a real whiz on the computer, no, not a nerd, very definitely not a nerd, beautiful like her mother, and very popular, and the colleges are going to be beating down her door to recruit her, she's perfect, a perfect kid, and anyway I really want for you to meet her someday, I really want to get you two together, no, look, I'm sure you two would hit it off, and it's important to me, very important, because, as I said, her mother and I, you understand, yes, yes, I wouldn't be surprised if we do, we're very serious about this, she's wonderful, she's perfect, I don't think I'll ever meet anyone that would compete with her . . . and anyway . . ."

I will stick that cell phone up your ass, Jimmy thinks. We'll see how proud you are of your goddamn cell phone after it's made the journey from asshole to throat.

". . . yes, look, I've got to sign off, I'm next in line for the coffee, I'll call you again . . . yes, soon, no you do always sound like you don't want to talk to me, never mind, how's your mother, a different shrink? but you're doing fine with yours? . . . and school?. . . you like your school? . . . any boyfriends? . . . not yet?. . . yes girlfriends are fine but there must be some boys in your class that you like . . . well, you will . . . gotta go . . . nice to talk . . . yes I love you too . . . don't forget--I definitely want you to meet Delawn . . . Delawn, yes, that's Franci's daughter, you'll love her, you'll want to be just like her . . . no, you will, trust me, okay, okay, good-bye for now."

The man puts his phone away and shoots Jimmy a proud smile, the smile of a man who is a success in his own mind, a winner in all the games of life.

Jimmy returns him a look that says, Don't speak to me. Don't even think of saying anything. I'm younger than I look and in better shape than you realize and the pain in my joints doesn't matter because I won't even feel it once I start hitting you.

The successful man's smile turns to a frown as he himself turns to the exotic coffee choices. Jimmy looks at his wife. She rolls her eyes and touches him lightly on the bicep. The man chooses a Sumatran blend and moves on. There are no multigrain scones or honey-bran muffins left. Jimmy shakes his head in disgust and goes to stand in line for a Diet Coke at Burger King.

The Corner Grocery

They call them "Junior Markets" out here. They are convenience stores whose sales are mainly beer and wine. Some of them have full liquor licenses, but the one on the highway just outside our tract never has. Maybe that's one reason it has a history of going out of business. Maybe it's because the mini-mall it's in is just too "mini"—the parking lot is so small that there's an exaggerated risk of fender-benders. Maybe some of its business overlaps with the donut shop next door. Maybe some of the previous owners didn't want to make money—maybe it was some kind of a front or they were involved in money laundering or something. I know a massive underground economy exists in my country, but its intricacies are as much beyond my comprehension as are those of the so-called legitimate economy. I have never really been a part of either. English teachers are not supposed to be a part of an economy—we are not supposed to understand economies. Those of us who understand money are regarded with suspicion, especially by the creative writing students. Fortunately, I have never displayed any signs of financial savvy. Obviously no one with any fiscal smarts would be caught dead shopping in such overpriced venues as neighborhood grocery stores.

I missed the corner grocery the last time that it was shut down, a period of over a year. I hadn't patronized it much because I was still drinking in those days and, as I said, it didn't stock hard booze or foreign beers or decent wines. It was pretty much of an emporium for Bud and Boone's Farm. And I'd purchased canned goods that had proved to be years past their sell-by dates. Canned chili does not improve with age. But it was good to have a place nearby if you ran out of toilet paper, Tylenol, or charcoal. And, the eternal optimist, I kept expecting it to improve, would drop hints of items I would love to see in stock, marketing suggestions that raised not the heavy lids of the listless, unenfranchised clerks. So I was mildly heartened to observe, driving by on the way home from a department meeting, a banner announcing its imminent re-opening under the proverbial new management.

It opened with almost as bare shelves as it had closed with, but the new man behind the counter, middle-aged, with an unostentatious moustache and a foreign accent, was much more eager to accommodate. "Diet iced tea?" I would ask, because I had now quit drinking and was under doctor's orders to lose weight, and he would take out a small pad and say, "I will get you some.' "Kellogg's Raisin Bran?" A week later there were stacks of it. "Non-fat milk?" "Tell me what you'd like and I will stock it for you . . .

"But what if no one else buys it?"

"You are a regular customer," he said; "You are one of my first customers. I want to stock things for my loyal customers."

That almost drove me away. I have never handled obligations well, as evidenced by my marital history, and I really couldn't afford to do all my shopping there, but I wanted to see the place do well, and the healthier items did appear on the shelves, and so I bit the bullet and pulled into the lethal parking lot more often than I really should have.

I always forgot to pick up a basket when I entered. I would end up at the cash register with boxes and bottles protruding perilously from my grasp. At first he would remind me of the baskets, bright red and donated, judging from the stickers, by the generous Marlboro people. Then he began bringing one to me. "Are you walking?" he would ask; "Take one home with you. If you ever want to pay with a check, feel free to do so. If you want to make the check for more than the amount, that's fine."

He even began to give me discounts: "I will only charge you a dollar for that," he would say. "Thank you, but you don't have to do that," I'd reply, but frankly I was grateful. I even took to timing my arrivals for when he was behind the counter. The quiet woman, younger than himself, also foreign, who sometimes worked in his stead, was perfectly polite but she did not know about the discounts. So if I happened in on her shift, I purchased only what was absolutely necessary.

I hope I have not given the impression this man was a fool. I never considered him so. He gave every indication of knowing his business, of understanding the value of creating good will, and of a core clientele. I had known bar owners who had underestimated these principles and others who had, to their detriment, forgotten them. After all, I did spend more there than I had ever intended to. And he knew by now, from my checks, that I lived in the neighborhood and taught at the local university. And, as with a restaurant, it is not good for a store to appear always empty. Success breeds success. And empty places are more apt to be held up. He was no fool.

On the other hand, he was not purely calculating either. He was of an ancient people who were capable of kindness. I figured he was either Middle Eastern or of the subcontinent. I thought the latter. When I asked him if he'd ever lived in England, he for the first time showed just the slightest hardness in his eyes, as if I were intruding where it was none of my business. Or perhaps he was remembering bad times there—I had forgotten tales of Paki-bashing. At any rate I hastened to assure him that I had simply been in England for stretches of time myself there, knew that there was a large Pakistani population there, and had in fact learned to eat Indian and Pakistani food there, which my wife and I now often drive the ten miles to Artesia for, the Southern California square-mile Little India. I recounted the first time I ate curry in Earl's Court, ordering the spiciest variety because I thought I'd been prepared for it by salsa, and almost sweated and hiccuped myself to death. We discussed regional differences of cuisine. He seemed reassured.

The next time I stopped by he told me he was going to prepare food for myself and my family. I didn't know whether he meant to invite us to dinner or to bring food to the store for us to heat at home. I was caught off guard and did not encourage him. I seldom socialize and my wife and I socialize with others together on only the rarest of occasions. I foresaw disasters. I shifted the conversation to the availability of frozen varieties of Indian food, and whether he intended to stock chutney. I'm sure I hurt his feelings—my implicit rejection of his hospitality may have been a serious rebuff in his culture, a painful loss of face. But to have done otherwise would have been merely postponing an eventual catastrophe. He did not speak of it again. I still feel bad about it, and I know I drew a line that day which neither of us would ever cross, but it was unavoidable. No doubt he had survived worse in his life. Probably he attributed it to race. It was not—I simply did not desire to cultivate family friendships with anyone. My private life is full and complicated and I need time for my work. Best friends have never been inside my house. It doesn't matter how he interpreted it. I could not be any other way. I am not at this point in my life interested in broadening my horizons or extending my social life. We would still be friends within the confines of the store. I was still a loyal customer.

We have skinheads in the neighborhood, kids from the nearby high school, or dropouts therefrom, or recent graduates. They gather together in what they no doubt think of as a gang, get drunk and hurl beer bottles at their backyard walls and threaten "to kill themselves a nigger." They are much more likely to be killed than to kill. No doubt they deal drugs to each other. Some of them end up in rehab programs. They are not intellectual luminaries. They do not add to the comfort of the neighborhood, especially since there is an interracial couple, graduate students, who keep a low profile, living across the street. Still, while I abhor racism, I understand the frustrations of these white kids and their feeling that they need to band together. The Blacks and the Chicanos, the Vietnamese, Cambodians, and Chinese all have their gangs—why shouldn't the Whites? Nor are Whites the only racists anymore. Their sense of being themselves victims of discrimination may not be entirely a matter of perception. The skinhead phenomenon is deplorable, and a source of tension in the neighborhood, but it was certainly predictable.

I saw a couple of carloads of them pull up in front of the corner grocery store one day. Some went inside and some stayed in the cars. From my own car I jotted down their license plates. I have a terrible visual memory but I did my best to notice a few of their physical details beyond the shaved heads. When they seemed to have been in the store too long, I got out of the car and went inside myself. But I found no sign that they'd planned a robbery or any violence. They seemed just to be shopping for after-school snacks. Maybe they were doing some petty shoplifting. It would be hard to keep an eye on all of them. A lot of that must go on in any corner grocery. My friend had a bemused expression on his face, but did not seem overly concerned.

For a while he had a couple of young people working there. But then one morning I saw in the newspaper that a string of places had been cited by the Alcoholic Beverage Control for selling to minors. The corner grocery was one of them. The young clerks ceased to be employed there. When I asked my friend about it, he said that they'd been unable to say no to their buddies. The offense would not be repeated. Signs went up warning juveniles. A sign also appeared of a store-keeper brandishing an outsized shotgun. The face of my friend was superimposed.

I realized I did not know his name. But I didn't ask. It would have seemed an intrusion.

He called me "Professor." I hate to be called "Professor" or "Prof" or "Doc" but I didn't correct him. He seemed to be comfortable with it.

He acquired a lottery machine. I had always purchased my Lotto tickets next door in the donut shop, but now I bought them in the grocery. The donut shop didn't need my business. I told myself that maybe it would change my luck. It didn't.

Then the new Lotto machine broke. It took the state three months to fix it. The corner store had a low priority on repairs because it didn't do enough volume.

"How are you supposed to sell more tickets with a broken machine?"

He smiled and shrugged. That seemed to be his response to setbacks in general. I could have used a little of that calm myself. I wondered what his religion was, if he was still religious. But I didn't ask. Whatever it was or wasn't, it probably boiled down to the religion of experience and maybe of genetic predisposition. I don't understand why we are the way we are any better than I understand economics, but I figure we are probably the way we have to be, the way life makes us. Those of us who survive at least. Like everyone else, I have my theories. I try them out, discard some, retain others, modify them as I go. And like all of us, I will die knowing nothing, certainly not whether I was born for a reason, or whether anything awaits me, or why I was the way I was.

I think, though, that I buy my Lotto tickets (now that the machine is finally fixed) at the corner grocery rather than at the donut shop because I like the proprietor more. The owners of the donut shop are Asian. I don't know if they are Japanese or Vietnamese or Chinese or Cambodian. I don't know if it matters. She is younger than he is. Neither of them ever smiles. The two of them are always in the shop. I'm sure they work incredibly long hours. I have read articles on how the members of the recent Asian immigrant communities help each other to make it in the donut business. They have become serious competitors to Winchell's. I admire this. I am from a background of Irish immigrants and they made it the same way, sticking together, helping each other out, working long, hard hours, saving their money, limiting their own horizons while expanding those of my generation. It is the story of America.

But the people in the donut shop never smile at me. They don't know how to joke with me. They try to get me to buy more Lotto tickets than I want. They try to get me to buy donuts when I don't want donuts. And their raisin-bran muffins, which are what I buy if I am buying only for myself, are, finally, not very good.

And so I prefer to buy my Lotto tickets from the man in the grocery store, although I do not think one can extrapolate from this to a preference for the peoples of the subcontinent over those of the Far East. The people in the donut shop may, for instance, have been boat people. God knows what they may have endured.

The Irish were, of course, boat people also. But not my generation. I do not, however, forget that I am not far removed from immigrant routes, even as I wonder, in the manner of the settled, the nativist, whether California can survive its current waves of immigration.

In England the Indians and Pakistanis seem preferred to the West Indians and Irish. They are considered more industrious. Perhaps they just absorbed more English culture in colonial times. Perhaps they were better treated by the English. Perhaps they have always been merchants.

Certainly not all the peoples of a Muslim provenance are as friendly to Americans as the man of the corner grocery store is to me. One thinks of the Iraqis and Iranians (although I have known many who hate their governments and love America). One thinks of the Algerians who picked my pocket in Paris. One thinks of the young Arabs who are alleged to have blown up the World Trade Center (after having been trained by the C.I.A. to subvert the Russians in Afghanistan).

No, we enjoy each other in spite of our origins, not because of them.

One thinks of A Passage to India, of Stoppard's Indian Ink, of Salman Rushdie.

I have not broached the subject of literature in the store. Who knows what can of worms I might be opening, what box belonging to Pandora.

I moonlight on occasion grading essays on a test of writing skills of those for whom English is a second language. As such I could be regarded as either an opener or a closer of doors. In reality I suppose I am both. I do not agonize over it. It is a good test and everyone connected with it strives to be fair. We do not know whose papers we are grading. The computer can tell if there is bias in our grading. If so, we are no longer invited to grade. The system has every possible guarantee of impartiality built into it. I do my job and cash my paycheck.

But I do not mention this avocation in the store. Who knows what relative may recently have been notified of a low score on this particular test. Some things are better left unsaid.

What we do banter about is the Lottery. I say, "I think I'm getting closer to winning.

"Tonight's jackpot is forty million."

"Maybe I'd better wait a week. I'm not sure that I could retire on forty million."

"What will you do with all your money when you win?"

"I'll probably spend most of it on Diet Pepsi." He laughs: "You'll be able to buy the Pepsi company."

"I wish I'd bought a little bit of it a long time ago."

"Yes, Coke and Pepsi are all over the world."

"Their only war is with each other."

"And maybe even then they share the pie. . .

"It's a big pie. Enough for both.'

"Oh well, good luck; I hope you win."

"I hope if I don't win that you do."

I mean it. I give him the thumbs up. He returns the gesture, seems to get a kick out of doing something so American. At that moment we are the Ebert and Siskel of Existence, giving two thumbs up to Life, its agonies and ecstacies and simple exigencies.

I had to quit eating Kellogg's Raisin Bran. A little too much fiber. I was getting cramps. The boxes sat on the shelf. The expiration date passed. No one else was buying them. I brought a couple of boxes home anyway. Tried to interest my kids in a healthier breakfast. They ridiculed that notion as they poured milk on their Captain Crunch. I gave the Raisin Bran another try myself. In a few days I was taking Immodium-D. The Kellogg's Raisin Bran remained stacked high and wide in the store. I tried not to glance in that direction on my way to the Diet Pepsi coolers.

The diet drinks, on the other hand, began to sell out. I seemed to have started something. He couldn't keep them in stock. He did not have a high priority with the distributors. I suspected him of going to his competitors to put a few liters on his shelves for me. He said, "You are such a good customer—you keep coming in even though so often I am out of what you like." "It's no big deal," I said. "What you don't have today, I'm sure you'll have tomorrow."

"You are my best customer," he said.

I said, "Just a second—I'm forgetting something."

I went back for a box of Kellogg's Raisin Bran, a half-gallon of bluish skim milk, and a package of

Immodium-D.

I don't know how well or badly that the store is doing. I tend to go in it off-hours, mid-morning, mid-afternoon. I haven't noticed any tell-tale signs yet, such as shrinking inventory. It's still pretty much a two-person operation. For a while there was an attempt to sell sandwiches, but that didn't pan out. My friend does not show worry, but of course he wouldn't. He would smile and shrug. He would have been through worse.

What worries me is that every store that has ever been in that location has gone under. There seems an inevitability to such things. Some locations can't lose; some can't win. Location, location, location. Like there will always be something strategic about Pittsburgh.

I keep shopping there, even though I know it's stupid. Not the major shopping—my wife does that at the supermarket. But the diet drinks, the Lotto tickets, the odds and ends that we run out of.

I tell myself that time is money, but what kind of money am I making with the time I save? I tell myself it's nice to have a place where I can cash a check, but there's an ATM machine almost as

close. I tell myself I've always preferred to hand over my money to a human being rather than a corporation. But this way I am handing over more of it.
When I'm a little short on funds, such as at tax-time, I swear off for a while, but then I miss the place. I even feel a little guilty. Which is ridiculous: I am my storekeeper's keeper?

I think that I'm just lazy.

This isn't a Big Story. It doesn't have a dramatic conclusion. No violence, death, betrayal. If there's a theme, you'll have to find it for me. It's a small part of my life, no doubt an even smaller part of his. As they say in the Mafia, "It's nothing personal, just business."

I don't know why I've even wasted your time, not to mention my own. It's just life.

A Kinder Gentler Hitler

It's an El Niño downpour on the Saturday morning of Valentine's Day, but Jimmy has braved the two-mile drive to the upscale shopping center to buy a box of Godiva chocolates for his wife. Now, remembering that they are out of milk and low on Diet Pepsi, he has pulled into their neighborhood convenience store.

The Pakistani man behind the counter—whether owner, manager, or employee Jimmy has never been sure—is an extrovert with whom Jimmy has carried on running banter over his chances in the state lottery and his over-consumption of phosphates. More recently the man has been trying to sell him on the superiority of a nearby Pakistani restaurant over the Indian restaurants of Artesia. Jimmy has tried the Pakistani place once and found it cheaper, homier—little more than a family kitchen—but inferior in every point of cuisine. Of course he hasn't told the garrulous clerk that, but he is finding it increasingly difficult to come up with excuses for not having returned there to sample the weekend biryani.

Today, however, he finds the vendor not merely in no mood for small talk, but in a veritable rage:

"Do you listen to the talk-shows?" he demands, gesturing over his shoulder at a staticky radio.

"Occasionally," Jimmy says.

"Americans know nothing," he says. "American history is bullshit."

"Perhaps," Jimmy says. "Perhaps all histories are. Then again, maybe not entirely."

"Let me tell you," says the man, his dark eyes blazing, "Americans think Hitler was a monster. That is because they have not studied Germany. They have not been told anything but what their government wants them to hear. Hitler only wanted what was best for his people. And if he had lived . . . the world might have been a better place."

A dripping customer enters and the clerk glares warily in his direction. The man goes towards the refrigerated shelves of beer in the back of the store. The clerk lowers his voice: "Americans don't understand what led to Hitler . . . . . Americans think they are loved by the rest of the world, but they are hated. America should mind its own business and keep its troops and ships at home."

"Many Americans would agree with you on that point," Jimmy says, taking his change.

"Yes, well, it is not the American people who are hated; it is just the government."

"I know," Jimmy says. "I've usually been treated very well in other countries."

It seems to be dawning on the man that he cannot expect to fulminate like this and work in a successful grocery store at the corner of Main Street, USA. He is making visible efforts to calm himself. He may even be wondering if Jimmy is by any chance a Jew. Jimmy isn't, but he's sometimes been mistaken for one.

"Have you been back to that restaurant I sent you to?"

"Not yet," Jimmy says. "We really haven't been out to eat much recently. Soon, I hope."

"Try the mixed grill."

"I will," Jimmy says, although he's virtually a vegetarian.

At home he recounts the episode to his wife. "Jesus," she says, "didn't you disagree with him?"

"Why bother? He'd just dismiss me as one more brainwashed American."

"Does he know you're a teacher?"

"No. That would make me one of the brainwashers. I just listened to him because I wouldn't have changed his mind anyway, and because I'd rather have a guy like that getting it all out than keeping it inside like a time-bomb, and because I'm a writer."

"He must really hate Jews."

"Maybe the Indians too. He's determined to get us out of their restaurants. He says their food is frozen."

"I'm not sure that place he sent us to had a refrigerator."

"I think it's just Clinton's threatening to bomb Iraq that has him pissed off."

"Will you go back?"

"Sure. I'll let a few days pass and neither of us will let on that anything was ever said. I wonder, though, if these people who hate America would be coming here if we weren't a world power."

"Like if Hitler had won?"

"No doubt the wretched of the earth would have been beating a path to his Ratskeller."

A Good Customer

By now Laurie remembers exactly how Jimmy likes his hair cut: short on top, shorter with the beard, and with the mustache scraped as close as she can get it without actually shaving it off. It's always the mustache that grows back first, tickling his nose and complicating his meals. Also, she has the female touch. He used to think he liked the maleness of barber shops, the gruffness or taciturnity, the matter-of-factness and stern opinions, but he notices that he's been getting his hair cut more often since he started coming to Laurie. He used to kid that a gentleman should not stint at paying thirty bucks a year for good grooming; but lately he's been calling for an appointment every couple of months. He feels a little sorry for the male barbers in the shop, and he figures they probably hate him for always insisting on their one female colleague . . . but maybe they should simply switch to styling women's hair. Not that Laurie is a "hair stylist"—Jimmy has no tolerance for any of that new-fangled nonsense. No, she just provides an old-fashioned halfhour cut with scissors and electric trimmers. No shampoo—he usually comes straight from a shower after swimming at the Y—and no stickum. She charges twelve dollars for the works and with the change from a twenty, he always adds the three singles as a tip. She always thanks him with what sounds like genuine gratitude.

It's not that she's a raving beauty, though she certainly is attractive, tall, with blonde hair and eyes that sparkle a light-blue. The hair goes nicely with the black gown that she always wears. She's kept her figure, has never mentioned any children. Her voice is quiet, soft, but not cinematically sultry. She seems to have no affectations. Maybe she can be a bitch on her own bad-hair days, but she doesn't bring it to the shop. She seems to genuinely like her customers.

They've talked enough so that she knows he teaches at the university, but even before then she never treated him like a homeless bum, the way a couple of the men initially had. They have one acquaintance in common, a music professor about Jimmy's age, although Jimmy suspects she may have known the man better than he does. Now, when he asks her if she's seen him lately she says, "He's been ill. I think he may retire."

"What's the problem?"

"Well, you know he has lupus."

"No, I didn't. He was kicking up his heels at that jazz concert that I saw you at."

"He was doing his best, but he hasn't been

really well for a long time."

"I'm sorry to hear that. He's an extremely talented guy."

Jimmy sort of dozes off again then as he often does, his eyes shut so as not to get any hair in them. They're limited in conversation anyway: a trip of hers to Palm Springs, what classes he's teaching, when he'll be able to drag his beloved long-haired son back into the shop. Jimmy never mentions his writing. Laurie seemed surprised when he admitted once that it wasn't all that long ago his hair was as long as his son's. Those days are receding faster than his hairline, though.

He opens his eyes to hear a young lady at the door asking Laurie if she's working late today.

"Unh-hunh. I have a five-thirty."

"Well, you're still working another couple of weeks, though, aren't you?"

"Till the first of the month."

"Then I'll see you before then for sure."

"What's this?" Jimmy says; "you're not leaving are you?"

"I think so. I was going to tell you when we were finished. I think I'd better take advantage of a chance I have to re-train on computers. My shoulder's never really healed completely. I'd still like to own my own salon someday. I may cut hair a few hours now and then in some other place while I'm going to school. The guys here will tell you how to get in touch with me when you call in—won't you, Phil?"

"Sure, Laurie."

Jimmy says, "I still have your number from when you were recuperating from the surgery on the shoulder, unless you've moved."

"No, I haven't moved."

"I'm glad for you if you want to do something else, but I'm sorry you won't be here."

"It's time I did a little something with my life. I'm forty-four . . . "

"I would have figured early thirties."

"That's nice of you to say, but, you know, I didn't take things very seriously in my younger years, lots of drinking, partying . . . "

"I did my share of that myself—those were good decades for it . . ."

"Yes, they were . . . they were fun while they lasted but they're over now."

"For me also."

"You have your teaching, though. And your family. Now it's time that I find something."

"These are good days not to be drinking and partying anymore, Laurie, because no one is. The ones who haven't quit are either dead or stick out like sore thumbs. I wish you the best."

"I appreciate it."

They finish up then, making sure the mustache is as short as possible, snipping a couple of ear hairs, removing the striped sheet without spilling hair on Jimmy's shoes and socks. At the register, Jimmy ritualistically pays and tips and promises he'll call her. "I'll never get my son back in here, now," he says.

"Give him my best," Laurie says.

Jimmy goes next door to a starving-student joint for spaghetti. Comfort food. He does not adjust well to change, and it's no small task to find another perfect barber. Something must have told him to come in a little sooner than usual. Maybe he just hasn't gotten over when he was in the hospital with pulmonary embolisms for three weeks and was overdue for a haircut and the Nurse Ratched Head Nurse wouldn't let him wash his hair, let alone shower.

Or maybe it's more than that. Forty-four? Jimmy is fifty-five. Eleven years difference. Nothing. He's really not too old for Laurie at all.

Maybe when he calls to see if she's cutting hair someplace else he should ask her out. Ha! Easier said than done. Ask her where? For a drink? Neither of them drinks anymore. For dinner? What would they talk about? His kids? Her computers? Her customers? It's unlikely they read the same books, go to the same movies. Music? Jazz? It's a possibility.

He doubts she thinks of him that way. Maybe if he weren't married. He might be a "good prospect" then. But he is married.

Probably she just appreciates his having been a good customer. A good lady barber and her best customer. No more and no less. What might Henry James have made of that?

A loss is what he would have made of it. A not inconsiderable loss. One of the many losses—more by far than consummated loves—of which our lives are largely made.

Determinants

She is, like Jimmy, in her fifties. Her hair, pulled back in a bun, is like his, greying. They both need glasses. She is as black as Jimmy is white. Her figure is compact for her age, or well corseted. Do women still wear corsets?

She leads him into the fitting room. She does not smile. She has always seemed to like him the least of any of the staff who fill his orders for prescription anti-embolism stockings--a sort of super-strength, super-expensive, custom-made support hose that one wears if one has been hospitalized for blood clots in the lungs. She is the only one who insists he leave a hundred-buck deposit when re-ordering. She was not happy when he kept calling to see if the last pair, delayed three months, were ever going to arrive.

He sits on the edge of the padded fitting table and pulls off the pair he is replacing, which have lost, as they do within two or three months, a great deal of their elasticity. "I think I need tighter ones next time," he says.

She stares at the wrinkles in the pair he is removing: "Have you lost weight?"

"I've lost about twenty pounds, I guess, since I was measured for these."

"You should get re-measured at least once a year when you're losing weight or gaining weight."

"Next time," he says, reflecting on the extra fifteen bucks a leg that will push the cost of a single pair over two hundred dollars. Non-durable prosthetics are the one thing his insurance does not cover.

She has removed the new pair from their plastic wrapping and is rolling one of them into the proper fold for donning,. She alights on a wooden chair across from Jimmy and gestures to her lap, her skirt pulled tight a few inches above her shiny, nylon-stockinged knees: "Right-foot first."

A bit surprised, Jimmy complies, his right heel coming to rest atop her firm lower thighs. She struggles to ease the stocking over his heel without tearing the stiff reinforced fabric, a fraction of an inch at a time. "This is the tricky part," she says.

"I know," Jimmy says. He would not have been so gentle, but that is no doubt why his stockings also wear through and wear out sooner than they should.

"They have to be tight to do any good," she says.

"I know."

"There we go," she says, as the stocking heel conforms to Jimmy's. It is easier to tug the top of the stocking gently up his calf.

"Over the hills and through the woods . . . he says ". . . to grandmother's house we go," she finishes

"We were raised on the same rhymes," he says; "I wonder if the kids today grow up on that one."

She shakes her head: "I don't know what their parents pass on to them today. Maybe nothing. I read every night to my babies, just as my mother read to us."

"My mother read to me," Jimmy says; "and then she had me reading to her. She was a schoolteacher." First grade, he remembers. At an all-Negro school. "I teach," he says, "and I find I can't take anything for granted anymore--can't assume that my younger students will have grown up on any of the staples I did."

She smooths the stocking, up his calf, removing a wrinkle or two. He does not have to wear the style that go above the knee, or, thank God, the pantyhose.

"Other one," she says, as one of his aunts might have, and he removes his right foot and settles his left on her tight-kneed lap, taking pleasure in the businesslike quasi-intimacy of their contact. "I doubt the young ones grow up on any of the songs and rhymes that I did," she says. "Of course they have their own music, if you can call it that."

"They certainly have more social life than we did," Jimmy says.

"Social life!" she laughs; "church was our social life."

"A young teacher at one of the high schools (a young, black woman, he thinks) told me if her students' parents are younger than thirty she tells the kids to have their grandparents come to see her--because the parents will have as many problems as their kids, or worse."

"I believe that," she says; "I don't even want to think about the drugs."

"I know that I don't have the answer," Jimmy says.

"The answer is the family," she says, "but what's the answer for the family?"

"I don't have that one either," Jimmy says.

"Well," she says, smoothing the stocking up his left calf, "these fit fine for now, but you make an appointment for re-measuring before we order the next pair."

"I'll do that," he says,removing his foot from her firm lap with some reluctance. "I guess I'll just wear these new ones."

"Might as well," she says, wrapping the old pair for him. He follows her out to the cashier observing the pull of her skirt against her hips. He thinks; a handsome woman is how we would have referred to someone still attractive at her age. Probably, he thinks, the business of my foot on her lap and rubbing my calves meant nothing to her. Maybe she's been a nurse. Maybe she's just tired of the whole business of bodies.

He writes a check for the balance owed and makes a point of checking her name-tag:

"Goodbye, Lareice," he says; "see you in a couple of months."

She glances at the check: "Goodbye, Mr. Abbey." She comes close to smiling, almost lets a hint of friendliness creep into her voice.

Back in the car, he thinks, It would certainly be understandable if she just has a blanket resentment of whites. Who knows what treatment she's had to put up with in her life. Maybe she's learned to hate men also. Race matters, gender matters, there is no denying that. It's just that he's sure they have a lot of things in common that matter also: children, middle-age, the way that their generation was brought up, a subtler code of sexuality--markers that traverse boundaries of sex and color. Maybe these are the denominators that, against all reason, have kept his wife and him together. He turns the key in the ignition, late for a literary meeting on campus. Hemingway said, at about Jimmy's age, that people were dying who had never died before. It seems to Jimmy that, all of a sudden, he is learning things he never learned before.

Nickel Popcorn

"Well," the old guy says to the two kids dressing in the same aisle of the locker room, "I suppose you boys will be real happy to get back to school again on Monday."

They're nice kids, not smart-asses, and they aren't sure what to say.

"When I was a boy," the old guy says, "I just loved school. I couldn't get enough of it. School was so much fun . . . never boring . . . and I was so happy to be learning so much—yes, I was always overjoyed when a vacation would come to an end."

This doesn't seem intended to require a reply, so the kids begin discussing what they think they'd like from the candy and snack machines.

"You boys should pack a lunch. Bring a nice sandwich and a piece of fruit in a brown bag."

"I usually do," the blonder of the youths replies, "but my mother forgot to go to the store last night."

"Oh, I see . . . but when I was your age I'd pack a nice bologna sandwich or a nice cheese sandwich and I'd spend the whole day at the Y."

I decide to let the two well-mannered boys off the hook, so I say I can remember doing that myself--bringing a sack lunch and staying all day at the Catholic Y, swimming, and playing basketball and, when I was a little older, using the weights. It was a cheap and handy form of babysitting for our parents too. Another one was dropping us off at the movie theatre for a double feature on Saturday afternoon and then again on Sunday.

"Oh, yeah, I remember that too. We'd get a quarter—fifteen cents for the ticket and a dime to spend on candy or popcorn and a coke."

I remember that it was sixteen cents' admission in my day, and I figure the old guy for at least fifteen more years than myself, but I guess that a single penny is a testimony to the lower rate of inflation in the '30s and the '40s.

"Roy Rogers and Gene Autry used to make about twenty films a year back then," I say, aware that I'm exaggerating slightly. I read they filmed them right up 395 at Lone Pine, in the shadow of Mt. Whitney."

"I liked the Our Gang comedies," the old guy says, and I can picture him—short, barrel-chested, proud of posture—as a character in those old flicks, a stern but kindly authority figure, a cop, maybe, or a football coach. Probably of German ancestry, maybe Polish, maybe Czech.

One of the kids gets up to go: "Nice talking to you," he says.

I wonder how long he'll stay that respectful of his elders, bombarded as he is by sitcoms and low-budget comedies. Ah well--the Little Rascals weren't always that respectful of their elders either.

"Those were good days," the old guy says, lifting his gym bag and heading for the door."

"Oh yeah," I say, although I also remember childhood having been a living nightmare, a reign of terror in which the sensitive were trapped between lawless bullies and repressive authorities.

As I go to weigh myself, I drop my locker key. The remaining boy retrieves it for me before I need to bend my stiff back. "Thank a lot," I say; "I appreciate it."

The scales impart good news--I've lost another pound. I'm the lightest I've been in thirty years. This Y is a good place, good for boys and good for men--and, nowadays, for girls and women as well. The benefits, it seems to me, are self-evident. And the bad eggs of other times and, maybe, of other Y's today, are not in evidence. It's not like the song by The Village People either.

"Listen," I tell this good kid as we both head for the door, "when we tell you about our sack lunches and our all-day sessions at the movies or the Y's, we're telling the truth. But when we tell you that we couldn't get enough of school, we're just bee--essing you."

Are You Ready to Rumble at the YMCA?

It's been the first truly Southern California day in April, and Jimmy is surprised that the pool wasn't packed for the two hours of lap swim. Emerging from the water at a minute before two p.m., he finds one other swimmer concluding a workout, a young guy who both surfs in the morning at Huntington Beach and swims here in the early afternoons at the four-laned outdoors but heated pool of the Y–after working the unloading truck for UPS. Well, he must sleep well when he does sleep. He's a quiet, well-mannered, naturally muscular young man who talks weather and sports in the locker room with Jimmy and listens to Jimmy's advice regarding his persistent dry cough, which Jimmy attributes to his having swum in the ocean after the recent heavy rains which empty bacterial waste into the mouths of the flood control channels, the concrete remnants of what were once rivers.

They've fallen silent now; tired, tranquilized by the exercise, the sun, the hot showers. Jimmy is pulling on the custom-made two-hundred-dollar

Jobst anti-embolism stockings which have for five years–in tandem with the anti-coagulant Coumadin and a regimen of exercise and diet that have resulted in the shedding of over a hundred pounds–prevented a recurrence of the pulmonary blood clots that almost consigned him to an early grave. He's fifty-eight now, no longer drinks, and if he stays out of accidents that could result in hemorrhaging--doesn't, for instance, smash his head on the end of the pool too hard or too often while doing his antiquated conventional backstroke--he should live a while. He tells the other old guys at the Y that if they can hang on just a few more years while the medical researchers develop gene therapies and harvest transplants, they just might live forever.

He's throwing towel, bathing suit, shampoo, and goggles into his gym bag when a young Chicano enters the locker room and says something to the surfer.

The surfer (no one learns names very quickly at the Y) says, helpfully, "No, the pool is closed. It closes at two."

"What I asked you," the slightly taller man continues, "is whether you just got out of the pool."

"Me? Yeah, I just got out about fifteen minutes ago."

"My girlfriend says you were bugging her."

"Your girlfriend? Do I know your girlfriend? There weren't any women in the pool with us."

"The lifeguard. My girlfriend is the lifeguard. She says you bother her, man, and now she's outside all upset."

"Bother her? I asked if she had to leave at two or if she'd be sitting there a while longer. I was hoping to get in a few more laps."

"She says you bug her, man. I don't like anybody bugging my girl, man."

The surfer is not a pretty-boy blond. His countenance is chiseled, his brow prominent--he could be an as-yet-unscarred pugilist. In a steady voice that betrays only the beginnings of adrenaline, he says, "Look, I wasn't coming on to your girlfriend. She said she couldn't stay and I said fine. But if that isn't good enough for you, let me finish dressing and we can step outside and settle this."

"That's right, man. I'll be waiting outside.'

And the boyfriend storms out of the locker room.

The surfer is clearly upset by the confrontation. "You know," he says, "she isn't even my type . . . seems nice enough. . . but I never even thought of her in that way . . . I don't know what her problem is. . ."

Jimmy is taking his time now, hanging back: "Just make sure that he doesn't pull a weapon on you."

There is no reply to that. It's food for thought.

Jimmy leaves the locker room ahead of the younger man. There's no one at the front desk–the receptionist must have stepped back into the office area. He sets down his bag and steps onto the big, old scales. A hundred eighty-three. He moves his feet around, tries to get it down to one eighty-two and a half. He prefers it to top out at an even one-eighty after the waterloss of the swim, even fully clothed. Got to ease the burden on the lungs, heart, circulatory system. He's been allowing himself too many handfuls of peanuts and raisins before bed.

What the hell, he decides he'd better wander outside with his fellow aquanaut. The other guy may in fact be armed or have friends. What ever happened to fair fights? In his thirty years in the bars, you always storrned out to back up a friend, but you didn't jump in unless supporters of the other guy got involved. There were unspoken protocols. Now the gangs and drug-gangsters operate under different codes, drive-by shootings for instance.

At first it looks as if there's nothing but unoccupied cars, but then the boyfriend jumps from the driver's side of a sporty, yellow, late-model vehicle parked next to Jimmy's Taurus. He's left the door open and from the passenger seat you can hear the lifeguard girl who's only been on the job a week sobbing and pleading, "Please get back in the car, please, I didn't want any of this to happen . . . please take me home. . . "

Jimmy opens the trunk and spreads his suit and towel to dry as the boyfriend gets in the surfer's face: "You see, you made her cry, listen to her in there . . ."

"Listen, man, you're the one who's making her cry. I already told you that I didn't say anything personal to her. Now if you think we have to fight, well, fine, I'm down with that, but there really isn't any reason for it and all your girlfriend wants is for you to get her out of here."

"I don't want you bugging my girl anymore, you get that, man?"

"You're embarrassing her, man."

Jimmy shuts the trunk: "It seems as if this is all just the result of an unfortunate misunderstanding."

The boyfriend glances over his shoulder at him. Jimmy thinks he may be about to tell him to stay out of it, to mind his own business. From the car the sobbing continues: "Please take me home. . ."

The boyfriend glares at the surfer, then abruptly gets back in the car, saying, "Just keep your mouth shut around her from now on, man."

He starts the car and backs out with surprising care, probably out of consideration for the expensive new car. There is no leaving of tread-marks on the asphalt.

The surfer moves towards his own aging vehicle, shaking his head. "Try to forget it," Jimmy says; "I'll see you tomorrow."

"Yeah, see you tomorrow. Thanks."

Jimmy waves him off. He re-enters the Y then,

thinking to spend a little time in the weight room, as he would ordinarily have done after getting off the scales.

The director, Mandy, who keeps up a running banter with him about his over-consumption of Diet Pepsi, is behind the counter now, as is the mild-mannered young receptionist. "Are you coming or going?" Mandy asks, "or can't you tell anymore?"

"There was just a little misunderstanding," Jimmy says.

"Oh, I guess I missed something."

"I was just making sure it got resolved. It did. No big deal."

"A man of peace," Mandy teases. "The poet."

"Peace or war," he grins, "whatever it takes."

In the weight room, though, the tendonitis in his right elbow is so painful that he doesn't even make it through his first set of curls. He's going to have to stick to the swimming for a while, although he has himself convinced that the heavy anthologies he hauls to and from his office and his literary theory class have done more harm than the weights. And he hates to have to lay off the lifting–it gives him the illusion of continuity with the Jimmy of thirty or forty or forty-five years ago. He's been lifting weights since seventh grade.

But it's a warm enough day, at least, for him to bask in the sun on the patio of the local Baja Fresh, enjoying fish tacos, a bean-and-cheese burrito, and a basket of chips with salsa fresca–his one real meal of the day–while re-hydrating and re-caffeinating from the Diet Pepsi spigot.

He feels sorry for the girl. She must be horribly embarrassed. He wonders if she'll be able to bring herself to return to her lifeguarding duties. He hopes her boyfriend doesn't take her home and beat up on her. Jimmy knows, though, that he probably would have made a scene himself when he was the boyfriend's age. He would have thought it was a matter of honor, just as the boyfriend obviously did. He hadn't caught on yet, as the young guy still hadn't, that the world had changed–well, middle-class America at least–and women didn't want you to fight over them anymore. Or thought they didn't.

It was sure a mistake for her to have said anything at all to him about "being bugged."

Jimmy smiles to himself. Maybe the surfer had put the make on her. Who knows? He wouldn't be apt to 'fess up to it now.

More likely she'd been feeling unappreciated and figured she'd make her guy just a little jealous.

Well, it has all turned out all right. Jimmy is feeling good about himself. He's feeling ten years younger, fifteen. He's making a point of not reflecting on how lucky he is that a fight didn't break out. One good blow to the head and he might be dying of a cerebral hemorrhage. But he isn't. He's experiencing the post-adrenaline, post-testosterone, euphoria. He's feeling like a man.

When he gets home, though, he'll warn his wife that if any gangs show up at the door she's to tell them he's skipped town without a forwarding address. And he won't discuss any of it in front of his teenage son to whom he has given explicit orders to steer completely clear of any such stupidly bullshit machismo imbroglios in his own life.

Of The People

When Jimmy sees the Van Dweller come into the locker room of the YMCA, he greets him with, "Hey, my man, was it fixed?"

"The fight? Of course it was."

"That's not the classic dive—to let your man get beaten bloody for ten rounds."

"The guy doing the battering didn't have to know the fix was in—he's always been a straight arrow—and the other guy apparently suffered a concussion in the third round—he may have forgotten he was supposed to go down sooner. The main thing is the odds dropped from 25-1 to 7-1 just before the bell . . ."

"I'll have to admit the loser's manager didn't look particularly upset afterwards."

"He probably had millions on the other guy. He's a mix of P. T. Barnum and Charles Keating, except there's never any element of uncertainty in his investments. He'll make another billion on the rematch."

"On the subject of upsets . . . how about my Yankees."

"I'll have to admit that really surprised me. I thought Atlanta might have had the greatest pitching staff in the history of the game. Well, the greatest since Wynn, Garcia, Lemon, and Feller anyway."

"I was from Rochester, you know, and Johnny Antonelli was the local hero. I don't think he even got into that series for the Giants. One of the first of the bonus babies so they couldn't send him down to the minors for seasoning. Later he owned a big tire store."

"The very first of the bonus babies was Tim Wakefield."

"You have an incredible memory."

"It's starting to go, though. I used to know, for instance, which pitching staff was the only one ever to have four twenty-game winners. It wasn't that Cleveland bunch--Lemon only won fifteen games that year. I think it was Boston or Baltimore--wasn't it Pat Dobson, Palmer . . . shit, I don't know."

"Where've you been the last few weeks--back in Detroit?"

"Yeah, visiting my father again. He thinks he's going to get out of the care facility he's in and come back home, but of course he never will. He can hardly breathe half of the time, let alone walk. It's sad to see, he was such a powerful man, such a tough guy. My sisters and I hope that he won't last much longer now."

"That's why I never pace myself in working

out. If I overdo it and get taken out by a heart attack, quickly and cleanly, great."

"The irony is, you'll probably get in such great shape trying to kill yourself that you'll live to be a hundred. But, you know, it's crazy—I'll go into a restaurant and buy the five-buck special that I don't really want instead of the seven-buck meal I'd had my heart set on. And afterwards I ask myself, why? What's there to spend the extra two bucks on? Clothes? Another CD? A fancy dessert so I have to walk an extra ten miles to burn off the calories? Start drinking again and fuck myself back up? I have everything I need because I've never really needed much."

"I do the same damn thing. Of course if I'm eating with my wife there's a method to my madness because I need to give her a strong example of frugality."

"Oh yes indeed, that's different. Wives often have a bit of difficulty mastering the concept of the Spartan existence. Middle-class wives anyway."

"It's got to be encoded in the DNA because a shopping trip seems to raise their spirits, whereas my idea of a perfect shopping spree is one where I find absolutely nothing that I want."

"A hundred-buck pair of shoes once a year maybe."

"Yeah, but even that depresses me--I've been wearing these same Birkenstocks for four years. I only own one other pair of shoes and those are for when it rains."

"You better keep eating the blue plate specials a while longer, pal. Put two bucks a day in the coffee can for fifty days."

"Yeah, I guess so."

The Van Dweller goes to brush his teeth at the sink, and Jimmy is about to pick up his gym bag and leave, when he hears his friend humming something that he takes to be "La Vie en Rose." This is a guy who has come up from the mean streets of Detroit, spent his working life in the military and construction, paid his dues in the A.A. . . . Jimmy waits until the other man has rinsed his mouth then asks, "The Little Sparrow?"

"Piaf?"

"You were humming 'La Vie en Rose'."

"I was? I love it but I haven't thought about it for a while. I wonder what put it into my mind. I had a double CD of something like forty-five of her hits but I loaned it out and never got it back."

"I visited her grave a couple of times in Paris. Same cemetery that Jim Morrison is buried in."

"Yeah? Now that might be worth a trip. But I guess it would be a wet ride in my van . . ."

"When'd you get turned on to her?"

"Oh, hell, I guess I must have been a little kid. They played her a lot right after the war."

"Yeah, I guess they did."

"She was in the résistance, wasn't she?"

"Apparently she used to entertain the French soldiers in German camps and carry messages in and out."

"You know who the great love of her life was, don't you?"

"You mean Maurice Chevalier?"

"Nah, that was casting-couch stuff. I mean Marcel Cerdan."

"I knew that but I'd forgotten it."

"The last real fighter to come out of France."

"They were a perfect match."

"And he was killed in, what, a plane crash?"

"That or an automobile accident. Something like that."

"Two tough kids up from the gutter."

"Two heroes of the people."

"Well," the Van Dweller says, "That's where art comes from, isn't it? From pain and suffering? From experience of life in its common denominators? And the greatest athletes also?"

"That's what they tell me," Jimmy says. "It sure worked for those two, Piaf and Cerdan. And even a privileged guy like T.S. Eliot suffered."

And as he heads out of the locker room to check his weight on the scales just inside the lobby, Jimmy thinks, That guy never ceases to amaze me. A new dimension every time I talk to him. The soul of a poet and an encyclopedic knowledge of sports. Fan of Cerdan and aficionado of Piaf. A man of the people. A good man. A very good man.

The Real Thing

We are drying off in the hollow, foggy shower room, and the Van Dweller asks me, "What was the greatest movie you ever saw?"

I say, "I used to think it was Shane. From the time I first saw it, as a kid in grammar school, until just a few years ago, I would have said Shane, and maybe I still would, but I haven't felt like watching it for a while–and I never used to miss a chance to see it. Maybe because it's so hard to be a hero in real life anymore--so little opportunity for physical heroism. . . maybe I'm just too old to fantasize that sort of role-that I could save anyone just by being tough. . . maybe because I'm the family man, with the mundane problems . . . not the single, skilled gunfighter free to ride in and out of situations, settling scores in an individualistic manner, outside the legal labyrinth . . . at any rate I've kind of shied away from seeing Shane in recent years."

"Shane was a great one all right. Alan Ladd, Van Heflin. . ."

"Jean Arthur, Elisha Cook, Jr. . . ."

"Jack Palance, Brandon de Wilde, even old

Edgar Buchanan. . ."

"Directed by George Stevens, music by Victor Young, from the novel by Jack
Schaefer. . .

"But ya know what one was always my favorite?"

"What one was that?"

"From Here to Eternity."

"God, you won't believe this but all those years I was touting Shane, if there was any film at all that could have competed with it for Numero Uno in my psychic life it would have been From Here to Etermity. In graduate school, I used to go around arguing that it, not Moby Dick, was The Great American Novel. No one took me seriously, of course. And did I ever tell you that one time I almost met the author, James Jones, in Paris?"

"No, you never mentioned that."

"I'd dragged my wife to eat choucroute garnie at this brasserie at the junction of the two islands in the Seine specifically because I'd read in another Jones novel, The Merry Month of May, about the student/worker riots of 1968, that that was his hangout, and sure enough he and his wife and another couple showed up, and he looked just like his pictures, a feisty, pugilistic bulldog, and the maitre d' kept referring to him as 'Monsieur Jeem,' and they got him a table right away."

"Did you speak to him?"

"No, I didn't. I was afraid he'd take it wrong, that I was interrupting a private night out with wife and friends, and that he'd say something nasty that would spoil for me these books of his that I had always loved. So I didn't. I just enjoyed being in his local pub and watching him be himself. I met Ginsberg once and it was a bad experience. On the other hand, I spent hours with John Fowles--he wrote The French Lieutenant's Woman--a couple of years ago, and it was as comfortable as could be, a great honor and a very simple and friendly and stimulating afternoon. A memory to cherish."

"You've had a really interesting life."

"No, I haven't. You have. I've been to London and Paris and met a few authors, but you're the one who has survived the streets of Detroit, the Navy, the Merchant Marine, construction work . . . living in your van now, living on the road, the life that the Beats only played at."

I leave unsaid the booze, women, drugs, mental hospital, lost kidney, A.A. . .. But he hears what I haven't said, because he replies, "I've just found that what Nietzsche said was right, that, however he put it, whatever didn't kill me would just make me strong. Resilient, anyway."

"And you see, you're quoting Nietzsche, and you've followed Bergman and Fellini, and you're using what Flaubert would call le mot juste--the perfect word–in this case, 'resilient'– and did you even have any college at all?"

"No, I didn't even graduate from high school. A lot of kids didn't in those days."

"So what turned you on to all these films and books and composers that are generally of interest only to the so-called intellectual types?"

"I just had a few good friends who went farther in academic pursuits than I did. Guys I'd played ball with and palled around with in the pool halls . . . the guys who transcended their misspent youth as I didn't. And they'd pass on to me the books they were reading or the jazz and blues records they were listening to--and there was a lot of that live, right in Detroit, of course, and we still went to films together, because they were still just students then, not successes in their careers yet . . . and you always cross paths with a few bright guys in the service . . . anyway, I just picked up a taste for some of the 'finer things' and it stayed with me. And now you pass along the tips. Oh, and I keep forgetting to bring you the duplicate copy I have of that Andrea Marcovici CD. You still haven't heard her?"

"No, I keep meaning to check her out at Borders or Barnes and Noble."

"I could be entirely wrong, but I really think if you've been a fan of Marlene Dietrich and Judy Garland and like cabaret in general that you'll be amazed at how good she is. I'll remember that CD."

We have moved to the locker room by now and finished dressing. The conversation has gravitated to ballgames and exercise regimens and a couple of good, reasonable places to eat. On the way out I step on the scales, decide to spend a few minutes on the bench press machine. The Van Dweller heads on out to the parking lot.

I haven't seen him since then. I guess it's been a couple of years. Maybe he finally moved to the couple of acres he'd bought near Kingman, Arizona. Maybe his sisters needed him in Detroit. Maybe he decided it was time to see Paris. I hope it isn't that he fell off the wagon. I hope the kidney problem didn't resurface in his only good one. I hope he didn't succumb to a late onset of depression, as seems so often nowadays–that would be hard for someone as alone as himself to battle, even with friends in A.A.

Because at a certain point I suppose some of us are apt to ask of Nietzsche, "Strong for What?"

Not that Nietzsche had such as the Van Dweller in mind. He wasn't all that democratic.

But I'm sorry that my YMCA friend isn't around these days, because I'd like to tell him that I finally saw Andrea Marcovici last summer. My wife and I drove up to the Pasadena Playhouse to hear her do an evening of Noel Coward called "Present Coward" to coincide with a production of Present Laughter. And since she is a regular now at the Algonquin Hotel's Oak Room, I could urge him to rent the video of Mrs. Parker and the Vicious Circle. And I could tell him how much I enjoyed this new English film Little Voice, with the girl doing these incredible impersonations of

Garland and Dietrich and Shirley Bassie, and Michael Caine doing an over-the-top reprise of Sir Laurence Olivier's bitter farewell in The Entertainer. And now there's a good movie about James Jones made from his daughter's memoir, A Soldier's Daughter Never Cries, and scenes are even filmed in that brasserie where the île de la cité meets the île st. louis. I could tell him to skip A Simple Plan, but not to miss Shakespeare in Love and Hilary and Jackie. I could tell him that the movie of The Thin Red Line is not James Jones. I'd tell him about having met Sean Penn at Bukowski's funeral and how there's a line in The Thin Red Line that's pure Bukowski, something about only feeling lonely when he's around people. I haven't seen The General yet, but it's next on my list.

I could tell him that I still haven't been able to watch Shane again, that, for instance, thare's a neighbor down the street who's been threatening our pets, and I'd love to put a bullet in his guts, but I don't have the option of riding out of town afterwards and, anyway, I still don't own a gun.

I miss my friend, The Van Dweller, and I hope that one of these days he shows up at the Y again. And if that is not to be, I hope that death, when it comes to him, comes quickly, maybe in the midst of a brisk walk along Lake Michigan, that he does not linger in poverty, disease, dementia, humiliation. That he dies as Pruitt did, not Nietzsche.

Sexy Beast Comes to the Multiplex

As Jimmy dutifully observes the scrolling credits of the English gangster flick, a frail old lady limps up the aisle on the arm of a man of AARP vintage himself. She catches Jimmy off-guard with, "Well, did you understand any of that?"

"About one word out of ten," he says.

"Being deaf at these art films sure sucks."

"It's not our hearing; it's the Cockney."

"What's that about their cocks?"

"Not their cocks," Jimmy says. "The slang. The dialect. Their accents. Like the way they say Heafrow Airport."

"I was there on my second honeymoon. My second husband had a cock the size of a kielbasa. But I wore him out in a year."

"Come on, mom," her son urges. "They want to clean the theatre."

'Johnny's a good boy," his mother says, "but his father had a wee-wee like a sweet pickle, so Johnny's had to eat a lot of pussy in his life. Nice shooting the shit with you, though, young fella. Keep your pecker hard. That new-fangled Niagara stuff works great. Best thing to come down the pike since the French Tickler."

Jimmy smiles at the screen until the Boroughs of Fulham and Hammersmith have been duly thanked and Dean Martin has concluded his serenade. Dean is dead now, and Frank too, and Jimmy has recently turned sixty.

The June Gloom Has Departed

"Just another day in Paradise," J. says, churning past Jimmy on her kick-board. "Doesn't Mrs. Jimmy swim?"

"Better than I do," he replies, "but she enjoys just having me out of the house, and I consider her the Number One Reason why I need a swim."

"Hah! You're funny, Jimmy."

The next time that they pass, he says, "The second reason is my job; the third is just to stay alive; and the fourth is your new two-piece bathing suit."

"It's so I can keep an even tan."

"The reason doesn't matter," he says. "Maybe I'll be inspired to break my Chippendale's out of mothballs."

"Ummm," J. growls; "I'd like to see that."

"Or maybe not," he concedes.

J. is forty-five, a little wider in the hips than when she left for Oahu eight years ago, but still beautiful. She is single and adores her Doberman, Freddie—surrogate son and much less bother than a husband—values her independence, enjoys a party.

Jimmy is sixty, has slimmed down, but knows he more than looks his age. Each day when J. arrives at the Y with her repertoire of flirtatious greetings for all the men, teenaged or octogenarian, Jimmy shoves his goggles up on his forehead and swims sidestroke facing her, even though it turns him towards the ultraviolet sun.

A Note From Home

When the good-looking, 45-year-old woman
at the pool, with whom toad is always
kidding around, announces that she is in
the market for a new boyfriend (her present
one of ten-years duration being unable to
tear himself away from his dog in hawaii
to join her in califomia),

toad replies,
(as all the other men have)
"look no further!"

momentarily caught off guard
(he being sixty),
she recovers with,
"i'm afraid i'll have to ask for
a note from your wife."

"okay," toad says, "but i'm going to have to
wait for the perfect time to present her
with a request of that nature."

the next time they find themselves

passing in adjoining lanes, she says,
"did you ask your wife for that note?"

and he replies, "she says she'll be only too
glad to write it, but she's wondering if it should
be more in the nature of a character reference
or of a permission to go on a field trip?"

a couple of weeks later, when she tells him that
(incredibly) she hasn't been getting asked out,
he suggests, "maybe there's just too much
paperwork involved,"

and when she's about to leave the next day
for a week in hawaii, partly to size up
how things stand with the old boyfriend,
toad says, "tell him there's a guy back here
who's practicing forging his
wife's signature."

she's one of a kind

she's bright, good-looking and, at 45,
could pass, like all the women who swim at the y,
for years younger.
you can add to that a gift for brightening
everyone's day with her always upbeat personali-
ty
and that playfully flirtatious quality
that makes any man from 9 to 90
feel a lot more like a man.

so i felt especially bad for her
the day she'd just been rear-ended while waiting
for a red light to change.
we'd talked about her history of back problems
when i'd discouraged her from using
the weight machines the day before.
i asked her if she had plans to get
x-rays immediately, and she said,
"do you know what kind of lawyer i work for?"
"i don't know," i said; "a good one?"
"yes," she said, "and specializing
in personal injuries."

two days later she arrived
at the pool pissed off:
"you won't believe what that guy who ran into me
is trying to pull.
he told my insurance company that i was fiddling
with some papers, took my foot off the brake,
and backed into him!
so i called him and said,
'mr. so-and-so,this is J. so-and-so.'
and he said, 'i can't talk to you; call my lawyer.'
and i said, 'no, mister so-and-so, you are going
to talk to me. i want to know why you lied
to my insurance company.'
'i can't talk to you; call my lawyer.'
'look, i saw the copy of the book of mormon
on your dashboard. aren't you ashamed of yourself
for telling such a blatant lie?'
'i can't talk to you. . . '
so i said, 'well, i just thought you'd want to know
that there was a witness to the accident.'
and he shot back, 'no, there wasn't!'
and i said, 'oh, yes there was;
there was one very important witness—
the most important witness of them all.'
'there wasn't any witness!'

'listen, mr. so-and-so, i respect the
religious beliefs all who actually
live by their beliefs,
but you are a hypocrite mormon.

the witness to our accident
was THE GOOD LORD!'

he gasped,
and i hung up."

i said, "i love it, jJ.;
i love that you did that."

and i swam away, thinking,
by the time jenny's through with this guy
he's going to think she did put her car
into reverse, and that she ran over his dick.

A Talking Dog

"A Talking Dog?" Jimmy says, as he side-strokes in the lane next to J.'s; "No, I'm not buying any talking dog stories."

"It's true," she insists; "I saw it and heard it myself. This guy has a talking Great Dane that he brings to the V. A. hospitals to entertain the men. They really appreciate anything that breaks the monotony of their days a little. I keep meaning to call and ask if they'd like me to bring Frankie over."

"Does Frankie talk too?"

"Not yet . . . but Frankie thinks like a human."

"What does the Great Dane say?"

"Oh, he can say video. He kind of draws it out real deep and rich, like Veee-deee-yooooh."

"What else?"

"Ice cream. Aiiiiiii-screeeeemmmmm."

"Tell me more."

"Hey, I never said the mutt was William Shakespeare. Basic: His vocabulary is still . . . fundamental."

"Can he say fundamental?"

"No he can't . . . and you're being mean . . . but

he can say I Love You."

"What does it sound like?"

"It sounds like Aiiiii-wuv-yooooo."

"J., have you noticed that video and I love you tend to sound a lot alike in Dogspeak? Is this Great Dane by any chance half-French?"

J.finally gives in and almost drowns with laughter: "You're awful, Jimmy, but Aiiiii-wuv-yooooo anyway."

"I wuv you too, J. And I'm sure the guys at the V. A. hospital will wuv Frankie. And if they don't, I know for sure that they'll wuv you. And really I'm just jealous because all my chocolate lab can say is Foooooood."

A Weekend Away

"How was the river" Jimmy asks J. when she returns on Monday from Laughlin, Nevada.

"Hot," she says, "very hot, but I came out a few bucks ahead at Video Poker."

"Did your doggie sitter take good care of Frankie?"

"Perfect," she says, "but you'll never believe what my Nosey Parker neighbor said to me. Right off the bat she had to tell me how many people had been in and out of my apartment while I was gone. 'That's fine,' I said, 'I told the girl that she could have a party if she wanted. They weren't late or noisy, were they?' 'No,' she says, 'but you'd better check to see that nothing valuable is missing.' 'Why is that?' 'Well, I hate to put it this way, but her friends were all Mexican!'"

"Did you tell her what a shock that was, this being Southern California and everything?"

"No, I just said, 'That's terrible: I left instructions she was only to let Big Black Men in.'"

"How'd she take that?"

"She stormed back into her place and slammed the door. The bitch. And my place, naturally, had been left spotless."

Jimmy laughs and to himself thinks, for the thousandth time, J, you're a classic."

New Year's Eve at Dr.Yee's Donut Shoppe

Jimmy Abbey did not go out this New Year's Eve. Well, he didn't go far anyway. He set out to drive a mile to Dr. Yee's (all-night) Donut Shoppe in search of a couple of raisin bran or fat-free muffins. His wife and son were watching the video of Twister and he couldn't get any reading or writing done in the same room with it. It was too cold this time of year to seek refuge in the other rooms, and he didn't want to seem asocial on New Year's Eve anyway. He had tried watching a little of the disaster flick, but it was impossible to take it seriously. The special effects reminded him of those racing car driving games that they used to have in bars back in the 70s, with obstacles and curves in the road flying at you on the screen as you twirled the wheel wildly to avoid crashes. And in the film the hero and heroine somehow avoided being hit by as much as a speck of dust although the very universe of sticks and stones was crashing through their windshield. So he'd convinced himself that he was either hungry or deserved a treat or something. After all, he had swum his archaic sidestroke for two-and-a-half hours in the heated (but not that heated) outdoor pool of the YMCA that afternoon. He was still chilled from it. And since his wife had been suffering for days from a stomach flu, they hadn't attempted their usual New Year's Eve spread of cheese, crackers, salads, and American caviar on slices of English cucumber from the deli section of the upscale supermarket. He'd quit drinking three years ago and, even when feeling well, his wife could seldom finish her single beer or glass of wine before bed. So Dr. Yee's made a modestly celebratory kind of sense.

Ordinarily he would have patronized the coffee house where his daughter had worked during her senior year of high school and where she'd been earning a few bucks while home from her first year of college. But it had closed early tonight and she was off to L.A. with friends for what was called a "Rave," an all-night deejay dance party. Of course her being out scared him, but she needed to be assured of her independence and adulthood now—and she had been responding responsibly to this new freedom. So he tried to look on the bright side: there would be at least no legal drinking at the Rave; she would be getting there before the bars closed, emptying their drunks onto the highways, and she would be returning near dawn at a time of minimal traffic; the young man driving was a good-hearted sort, and his car's engine had emitted no clearly symptomatic noises as he drove off. The time had come for Jimmy to relinquish control as a parent and to trust in his daughter's basic goodness and the upbringing she had received.

He had given the dog a tranquilizer to help it cope with the guns that would be discharged into the air of the inner city at midnight. He should have taken one himself.

It's a comfort to him that already there are almost no other cars on the road. The bad news is that the one car in front of him is swerving badly, its driver clearly and prematurely drunk out of his ass. Jimmy hangs back until the fool careens up a ramp to the freeway, where Jimmy discerns the flashing lights of police supervising the clearing of a collision.

He recalls the New Year's Eves of his drinking days; the best had been at neighborhood bars or parties among friends. No ridiculous expenditures of money. No "are we having fun yet" hysteria. Just people set on abandoning their inhibitions for a night of flirtations or stolen kisses. A place to stay over or someone to drive him home. The varieties of alcohol had been such an adventure in those early days, such a refuge from his uptight puritan Catholic boyhood. And, in his mature years, such an anodyne for sexual guilt. Eventually, of course, it had gone bad, and he is glad to have put it behind him in time. But there is a flicker of nostalgia for Eves past on which he might be in the arms of someone else's hot-breathed, momentarily liberated wife.

Earlier in the day his high-school son had asked him, "What's the big deal about a New Year's anyway?" And Jimmy had considered the question and replied, "It's just a good time to take stock. Remind oneself of the events, good and bad, of the past year, and make plans for the new one . . ."

"Do you make New Year's resolutions?"

"Not so much anymore. I have a pretty good idea where I'm going now."

A new worker hurries from the kitchen to the counter of the donut shop. An Asian, of course, most likely in his thirties, thin, wiry, in surprisingly high spirits considering that Jimmy can detect none of the tell-tale signs of alcohol or drugs. "Are you having a wild New Year's Eve?"

"Oh sure," Jimmy says, "can't you tell?"

"What can I get you?"

"Which of these muffins are the fat-free ones?"

"Oh, I don't know—maybe these . . . the banana nut and the blueberry . . . maybe none of them."

"You don't know."

"I haven't learned yet. I am new, you see. And I am the night baker; these were baked by the day baker."

"Well, give me one banana nut, one blueberry, and one raisin bran . . ."

"Three muffins. You will eat them all yourself?"

"I will eat them all myself. It is my way of celebrating the New Year."

"It does not matter if they are not fat-free this one night. You must enjoy them. Something to drink . . . a Bud? You like a Heineken perhaps?"

Jimmy laughs. Of course the donut shop does not sell beer. "No beer tonight," he says; "I'm afraid I drank up my life's allotment of beer a few years back . . ."

"Oh, I see, you were a bad boy. And now you have to be a good boy. No matter: you will enjoy your muffins. All three of them."

"I will enjoy all three of them. Very much I will enjoy them."

"And I wish you a happy New Year."

"As I wish you."

The cheerful man, still smiling, goes back to his kettles and ovens as Jimmy returns to his car.

Pulling back onto the highway, Jimmy can't help thinking what a clean, well-lighted place the donut shop is, and how, unlike the café in Hemingway's story, Dr. Yee's never closes. Hemingway would have liked that. A refuge from the storm. A beacon in the fog. A place you could go when you didn't want to be alone in your room.

Although he would have preferred to be able to get a drink there.

Hemingway would have liked the good-natured worker too. The professors liked to focus on Hemingway's enemies, but those were literary enemies, and writers never get along with each other, not for very long. Among the common people of the world—the waiters and bartenders and fishermen—Hemingway had thousands of friends. Hemingway had been a good guy. The professors who wrote about Hemingway, most of them, were not good guys. It was as simple as that. Almost. They were jealous of Hemingway. They would have given anything to be Hemingway. But a Ph.D. from an Ivy League school could not make you Hemingway. That struck them as cosmically unfair, the worst imbalance in the entire universe. That nothing they could do or buy could make them Hemingway. They could suck every dick in the literary world, lick every pussy, and they still would not be Hemingway. It just wasn't right.

And Hemingway had laughed at them for this. He hadn't liked them, hadn't even curried favor with them, hadn't needed them. Bukowski hadn't either. But they would both have liked the night-shift baker / counter man at Dr. Yee's. His ebullience. His fearlessness—such places were held up, their workers murdered, every night of the week. God knows what the man may have suffered in his native country or on the voyage to America. Or what they paid him here, what conditions he lived in, how much of a family he may have to support. Some had been tortured and imprisoned in their countries. Some had come as boat people, seen their women raped by pirates. Whole families had been wiped out in places like Cambodia. Some were held as virtual slaves in sweatshops in this country. Unthinkable miseries, deprivations, humiliations, persecutions, setbacks. And yet they had been coming since the 19th century. Not just surviving but getting ahead. Sacrificing to send their sons and daughters to the finest universities, into the elite professions. Becoming Americans, loving America. And so many of them managing somehow not to hate.

And tonight wasn't even their New Year!

At home Twister is over. His son is reading in his room and listening to space rock. The dog is howling but less frantically than if he were not medicated. Jimmy settles in to his muffins and diet coke. He surfs the channels with the remote, but can't even find a rendition of "Auld lang syne." He's always loved that song, still does. His friends are starting to fall by the wayside, first Bukowski, now Marvin Malone, the legendary editor of the Wormwood Review who, for thirty-five years, was Jimmy's editor, friend, father-confessor, father-surrogate, ideal reader, moral support. Great holes are being left in Jimmy's life.

Bobbie Burns was a man of the people, like

Hemingway, no matter how the professors try to turn him into a sophisticate.

Hemingway used to say, near the end of his life, "People are dying this year who never died before . . ."

And what did Hemingway die of? Of cowardice and phoniness, as the gloating professors would have you believe? Of alcohol? Depression? His history of head injuries? Of hemochromatosis as Susan Beegel persuasively argues? Did J. Edgar Hoover or the CIA have a hand in the decline or demise of the Hemingway who was, with his enormous international prestige, anti-Batista and a potential supporter of Castro?

No, what killed Hemingway was simply what kills everyone.

Life killed Ernest Hemingway.

Jimmy goes to hug his son goodnight: "I hope it's a tremendous year for you," he says, "for your music . . . for your writing . . . I hope you have wonderful times with your friends, and read a lot of great books, and that we have good times together, see some good movies, maybe go to some concerts, and that you do well in school without it taking too much of your time. Oh, yeah, that you get your driver's license. You're doing just great and I love you very much."

"I love you too," his son says, "and I hope you

have a good year also."

His daughter arrives home early: "We never got to the Rave. The police had already shut it down and there was practically a riot outside the Convention Center so we drove to the top of a parking garage and watched it all for a while and then we came home. But we had to drop the others off first."

"What was the trouble?"

"Some kind of supposedly herbal-high drink got passed around and a whole lot of people collapsed and had to be taken to the hospital."

"Jesus. Well, you did the right thing. I'm very proud of you. And I'm very glad you're here."

"Happy New Year's."

"Yes . . . yes . . . Happy New Year's to you too."

Jimmy rolls over to go back to sleep. He will sleep well now. The dog has even shut up finally. Maybe he and the dog will both have happy dreams this year. Maybe it will be a wonderful year for everyone. Maybe the night-shift man at Dr. Yee's (24-hour) Donut Shoppe will still be smiling next New Year's Eve.

The Fool of Los Coyotes Heights

Those aren't cameras," Jimmy's wife says.

"What else could they be?"

"They're sensors. They allow the police and firemen to control the lights as they approach them on emergency responses."

"Are you sure about that?"

"No, but I am sure that they aren't cameras. I saw the pictures of the cameras they're going to install and they're much bigger than that. And the intersection that they're targeting is two blocks over."

"Shit, shit, shit, shit shit. . ."

"What's the problem?"

"I warned Giovanni about this intersection yesterday. He said he'd spread the word among his diners. You know how gregarious he is, how he always goes table to table."

"Well, Jimmy, I don't think Sicilians like to be embarrassed like that."

"I know they don't, Brenda. And Giovanni's an American. He's only from Sicily."

"So was Al Capone. So was. . ."

"All right. Enough."

Jimmy drives glumly towards their tract home in the suburbs, but before they get there he relents. "Okay, I'll tell another one at my expense. This morning when I called the Los Coyotes Animal Clinic about the dog?"

"Yes?"

"Well, I went on about how its eyes were goupy but we didn't know if it was necessary to bring it in because conjunctivitis in humans usually cures itself and how old the dog is and how it lives in the back yard . . . and all of a sudden the girl on the other end of the line interrupts me with, 'Sir, are you sure you were calling the Los Coyotes YMCA'?"'

"0h, no . . . that's your Y."

"I know, I know."

"Had you given your name?"

"I'm pretty sure I did. And the dog's."

Brenda is laughing so hard that Jimmy can barely negotiate the car to the curb: "And the dog has such a dumb name."

"I know, I know."

"Poopsie."

"Brenda, that's enough. I know the dog's goddamn name."

"Oh well," his wife tells him, holding her aching sides, "after the embarrassment you've no doubt caused Giovanni, your days of humiliation at the Y are severely numbered anyway."

photo credit: Vanessa Locklin

Gerald Locklin has published over one hundred volumes of poetry, fiction, and literary essays including Charles Bukowski: A Sure Bet, Go West, Young Toad, Candy Bars and The Life Force Poems (Water Row Press). Charles Bukowski called him "One of the great undiscovered talents of our time." The Oxford Companion to Twentieth Century Literature in the English Language calls him "a central figure in the vitality of Los Angeles writing." His works have been widely translated and he has given countless readings here and in England. He teaches at California State University, Long Beach.